# ONLY YOU

# DEBORAH GRACE STALEY

**THORNDIKE**
**CHIVERS**

This Large Print edition is published by Thorndike Press, Waterville, Maine, USA and by BBC Audiobooks Ltd, Bath, England.
Thorndike Press, a part of Gale, Cengage Learning.
An Angel Ridge Novel #1.

The text of this Large Print edition is unabridged.
Other aspects of the book may vary from the original edition.
Set in 16 pt. Plantin.
Printed on permanent paper.

**LIBRARY OF CONGRESS CATALOGING-IN-PUBLICATION DATA**

Staley, Deborah Grace.
   Only you / by Deborah Grace Staley. — Large print ed.
      p. cm. — (An Angel Ridge novel ; no. 1) (Thorndike Press large print clean reads)
   Originally published: Smyrna, Ga. : BelleBooks, 2004.
   ISBN-13: 978-1-4104-2108-1 (alk. paper)
   ISBN-10: 1-4104-2108-2 (alk. paper)
   1. Tennessee—Fiction. 2. Large type books. I. Title.
PS3619.T348O55 2009
813'.6—dc22                                              2009030477

BRITISH LIBRARY CATALOGUING-IN-PUBLICATION DATA AVAILABLE

Published in 2009 in the U.S. by arrangement with BelleBooks, Inc.
Published in 2010 in the U.K. by arrangement with BelleBooks, Inc.

U.K. Hardcover: 978 1 408 45760 3 (Chivers Large Print)
U.K. Softcover: 978 1 408 45761 0 Camden Large Print)

Printed in the United States of America
1 2 3 4 5 6 7 13 12 11 10 09

# ONLY YOU

This one is for Betty Grace. Happy birthday, Mom.

# ACKNOWLEDGMENTS

If thanks were flowers, you'd all be showered with bouquets. To Mom and Dad, Sherman and Betty Grace, for instilling in me the notion that anything is possible. Fred and Ethan, your love and support give me wings. Will the real Dixie please stand? Janene Satterfield, you are my definition of a true Southern Woman! Eternal thanks to Debbie Ledgerwood for encouraging me to create Angel Ridge. JoAnn Ross, you've helped me grow up as a writer. Thanks for being such a great role model. To Susan Sipal for helping me see things more clearly.

And last, but by no means least, to my writer buddies who inhabit the Mother Planet. I don't know what I'd do without you! To Kathryn Falk and *Romantic Times BookClub* for giving me a great start on this journey. To my RT buddies, The Society of the Purple Prose, especially Patty Harrison, Mary Schaller, Karen Smith, Linda Castle, and Gwynne Forster for your support and unshakable belief in me.

# WELCOME

Hey, ya'll. Dixie Ferguson here. I run Ferguson's Diner in Angel Ridge, Tennessee. Population three hundred forty-five. Even though I wasn't born here, well, I call it home now, and most of the locals accept me as one of their own. Let me tell ya a little bit about our corner of the world.

It's a picturesque town in the valley of the Little Tennessee River, established in 1785. In the early days, its first families — the McKays, the Wallaces, the Houstons, the Joneses, and, of course, the Craigs — staked their claims on hundreds of acres of the richest bottom land anyone had ever seen. They built large homes near the meandering river and operated prosperous plantations. Well, all except for the Craigs. They were traders and craftsmen. Men of commerce, as it were. Meanwhile, the town developed above the river on a high ridge.

In the early 1970s, the Flood Control

Board came in and bought up about all of the property along the flood prone river, and those stately homes that some called relics of a bygone era were inundated in the name of progress. But those who built more modest houses near town up on the ridge, well, their homes are still standin'. Of course, the families who lost theirs to the newly formed Tellassee Lake moved up to the ridge as well and built elaborate Victorian mansions such as this quaint little town had never seen.

Most of the families I mentioned earlier are still around. These folks are hardy people. Why in all the time they've lived here, they've endured Indian attacks, floods, divided loyalties in the Civil War, and yes, even feuds. The older folks are still marked by the hardships of the past, but the young people of the town hope to move beyond old hurts to create a new generation made strong because of their roots, yet free of the past.

After all the years I've spent behind the counter at Ferguson's, I could probably tell ya'll a story about near everyone in town. But we only have so much time, so I'll narrow it down to just two for now.

This is a story about coming home. It's also a story about acceptin' folks for who they are. You could say it's a story about a librarian and a handyman, but I say it's a story about findin' love where you'd least expect to. Ya know, those kinds of things always seem to happen when you open up your heart to possibilities. Of course, a little help from our hometown angels and yours truly don't hurt none either!

So, come on along to Angel Ridge. Sit a spell and enjoy.

# CHAPTER 1

A man is not where he lives, but where
he loves.

Latin Proverb

It was one of those days. Mid-May . . .
spring on the cusp of summer. A rare day.
One with the bluest of skies dotted with cotton ball clouds and the temperature perfect
with a cooling breeze blowing up from the
lake. No one could ask for a better day, but
not a thing had gone right since Josephine
Allen's feet had hit the hardwoods of the
turn of the century Victorian that had been
her childhood home in Angel Ridge.

Josie had lived on the ridge up until she'd
gone away to college. She'd been away for
nearly seven years; but now she was back.
The town had chosen her as the "right
person" to take over the directorship of
Angel Ridge's most prized possession: the
Angel Ridge Library. Expectations were

naturally high for the town's golden child.

So far, she had not delivered.

It had begun with the pronouncement by her parents that they would be moving to a retirement community in Florida. The house, of course, would be hers now. Whether she wanted it or not. Not an option. And then there were the problems with the cataloging program that had been keeping her at the library every night to all hours.

So, she'd awakened this morning to no power, no alarm clock, no curling iron, and no hot water. After a late night at the office, was a hot shower too much to ask? She did the best she could with her appearance under the circumstances. No time to check the fuse box. She'd barely make it to open the front door of the library by eight. There were probably people already lined up on the steps anxious to hit the genealogy room. They always came early and stayed until closing.

Two hours later, things at the office weren't going any better than things at home.

"Dr. Allen? Cole Craig on line two for you. He says it's urgent."

Josie turned from her computer screen to look up at her secretary standing in the doorway of her office. "Thank you, Teresa."

Josie removed her wire-rimmed glasses and pinched the bridge of her nose. The library's out-dated computer system had crashed twice already today, and it wasn't even lunchtime.

Cole Craig. Cole Craig. The name rang a bell, but her brain was so scrambled, she couldn't match a face to it. She punched the button below the blinking light on her phone, picked up the receiver and said, "This is Dr. Allen. How may I help you?"

"Is this Josie Allen?"

The deep voice laced with a smooth southern drawl flowed through the telephone line to caress her ear. Chill bumps raced up her arm. "*Um — Yes,*" she managed through a suddenly constricted throat.

"This is Cole Craig. I'm sorry to bother you at work, but there's a problem at your house."

She frowned. She knew that, but just how did this person also know? "A problem?"

"Yes, ma'am. I was cuttin' Miss Estelee's lawn this morning. I had just cut it on Monday, but with all the rain we been havin', I decided to cut it twice this week. So, when I stopped by her place today, like I always do on Thursdays, I decided to cut her grass again, and when I was around on the side of the yard closest to your house, I heard water runnin'."

Josie could have gotten lost in the verbal maze, but instead, a bell went off in her head. Cole Craig. Of course. How could she ever forget him? A couple of years older than her, they'd gone to middle school together, but she'd heard he had to drop out of high school to help his ailing father keep their farm going. He'd never finished school, but he, like his father and grandfather before him, had not only supplied the town grocer with produce and the butcher with meat, but had also built houses for the poor and rich alike.

The Craigs were the founding family of Angel Ridge, much to the chagrin of the more prominent McKays and Wallaces. The Craigs had never been rich, but they'd worked quietly and with dignity in the community for generations. They were always the first to lend a helping hand around town. And everyone knew that Cole Craig was good with his hands.

"I hope you don't mind," he continued, "but I looked around a little and noticed water running down your sidewalk to the street, so I took a peek at your crawl space."

"Of course I don't mind. What did you find?"

"Well, it was just what I thought."

Josie waited. When he didn't supply any further information, she prompted, "What was that, Mr. Craig?"

"Oh, please. Call me Cole."

That odd warmth poured through her veins again. He had the most lyrically beautiful voice for an uneducated man. Cole. The name seemed incongruent with the voice. "What did you find?"

"A busted pipe."

"Oh, my." She involuntarily winced at the slang usage of the verb "to burst."

"I went down to the water meter and shut off the main. But there's no tellin' how long that thing had been sprayin' water. You've probably got some wet floors in your house."

"Yes, I'm sure you're right."

"I'd be happy to fix it for you, Jos— *um* . . . I mean, Dr. Allen."

He said the word "doctor" like it felt foreign on his tongue. It was probably difficult for him to reconcile the young girl he remembered to Dr. Josephine Allen, Director of Library Science to the Angel Ridge Library. She wondered if he'd ever set foot in the library? Probably not.

"That's kind of you, Cole, but I'm sure you had other things planned for today. I'd hate to put you behind."

Josie hadn't been back in Angel Ridge

17

long, but she knew that Cole Craig was in demand. Anyone in town who had something that needed fixing called Cole. She smiled. Her memories of him were of a big, beefy boy who'd always been kind to her despite the teasing she'd received in school for her bookwormish ways.

"Oh, it's no trouble, ma'am. That place of yours must be a handful since you don't have your folks around tendin' to things. It was a terrible loss for the town when they moved away. They were fine people."

He made it sound as if her parents had *passed* away, when what they'd really done was left her holding the bag in the form of a drafty old house that needed constant attention. "Yes, I don't really have the time or the knowledge needed to keep up such an old house."

She'd thought of taking a condo in Maryville, but her parents had nearly had heart attacks when she'd suggested it. So, she'd resigned herself to living here. It was her home, after all, and she did enjoy the short walk to work. How many towns remained in America where one could walk to work?

"You're lucky to have it. They don't make 'em like that any more."

Josie wouldn't know. How she longed for

a nice, cozy place that was warm in the winter with no yard work in the summer. Something that wasn't in the middle of a town where she'd always been under a microscope and had never fit in.

"I'm more than happy to oblige," he was saying.

She couldn't help smiling at the quaint turn of phrase in Cole's slow, southern drawl, even though she wasn't quite sure what he meant by the statement. "I'm sorry. You're happy to oblige?"

"Sure. I can crawl up under the house and have a look at that pipe, then I could run down to the hardware and get what I need to fix it. I expect I'll need to get a look inside to see if there's any trouble in there, though."

"Of course —"

"I'll just mosey on into town to get some supplies, then. If you could swing by here at lunch to let me into the house?"

Josie looked at her watch. "I could leave now —"

"Oh, no ma'am. There's no need for that. It'll take me a bit to get what I need and come back here to start work on it. Noon'll be fine."

"Noon it is then. *Um, Mr. Craig?"*

"Cole, please. Mr. Craig sounds like

19

somebody's daddy."

His warm, soft chuckle heated every ounce of her blood. The images running amuck in her mind weren't the least bit fatherly.

"I'll call Mr. DeFoe at the hardware and ask him to bill me for the supplies."

"No need. We'll settle up later."

"You're sure?"

"Yep. See you in a bit."

The line went dead. Josie replaced the phone and sat back in her leather chair. A burst water pipe. Her house was probably a mess. She should go assess the damage, but Cole seemed to have everything under control. She rolled the mouse to disable the screen saver on her computer, and the stupid thing locked up again.

If only Cole Craig could work his magic on her hard drive. . . .

"Afternoon, Miss Estelee," Josie called up to the elderly woman rocking away the afternoon on her front porch.

Miss Estelee had been the Allens' neighbor for as long as Josie could remember. And for as long as she could remember, Miss Estelee had taken tea and cookies on her front porch at noon, weather permitting.

Josie shaded her eyes against the noonday sun. "How are you today?"

"Oh, can't complain. No need, even if I was want to." She laughed. "Can I offer you a cookie?"

Josie smiled. Miss Estelee's homemade sugar cookies were the best, but she said, "No, thank you. I'm meeting someone."

"That nice young man who cuts my grass says there's trouble at your place."

"Yes, ma'am."

"Well, if it can be fixed, Cole'll fix it. But be careful."

Josie squinted into the bright noonday sun at her neighbor. "Careful?"

*"Mmm."* Miss Estelee took a bite of her cookie, rocked back in her chair, and gazed up at the clear blue sky. "Them angels is a workin' mischief today." She shook her head and cackled, then slapped her knee. "Might have a mind to take you in hand, missy."

"I'll take that under advisement, Miss Estelee," she said indulgently. "Good afternoon."

"Afternoon."

Shaking her head, Josie walked around to the side of her house. Poor Miss Estelee. No one really knew how old she was, but she'd been ancient for, well, forever. The sweet old lady seemed to always be telling

21

anyone who cared to listen of the exploits of the angels living on Angel Ridge.

Curious, Josie had done a little research in the town archives at the library about these "angels." Legend had it that an angel appeared to the first Craig settler back in the late 1700s and told him to name the town Angel Ridge. The early settlers built forts to protect themselves from the Indians in the area, and the story went that when the Cherokees threatened an attack, some of the locals took refuge in the Craig Fort.

After Cole's ancestor agreed to name the town Angel Ridge, the tale went that the Cherokees would pass up the Craig Fort and attack the McKay Fort instead. Funny. There'd always been bad blood between the McKays and the Craigs.

Accounts of the attacks on the McKay Fort were well documented. But the legend about the angels appearing to the Craigs? Well, that's all it was . . . a legend.

Dear, sweet Miss Estelee. But who could argue with her? She *was* the town's oldest resident.

"Afternoon, Josie Lee."

Boy, that brought back memories. No one had called her that since . . . Josie turned the corner at the back of her house, and there he stood. Cole Craig.

"I'm sorry. It's Dr. Allen now, right?"

All she could do was nod. Gone was the beefy teenager she remembered from middle school. In his place stood a tall, muscular man with blond hair that grew past his shoulders, chiseled features, and eyes that rivaled the blue of the sky. The mud splattered on his faded jeans and tan t-shirt complimented his rugged good looks.

"Sorry to call you home in the middle of the day like this."

Josie cleared her throat and found her tongue. "I'm the one to be thanking you. I'm fortunate that you were nearby and observant enough to see that there was a problem."

A lazy smile pulled at the corner of his mouth, and a mischievous light danced in his clear, blue eyes. "Miss Estelee would say it's them angels workin' their magic."

The man was strikingly beautiful. For a moment, Josie forgot to breathe.

Cole moved forward and touched her arm with a gentle hand. "You all right, Dr. Allen?"

She blinked. She hadn't been this tongue-tied in — well, she couldn't ever recall being speechless in the presence of a man. This was just Cole Craig of the blue collar Craigs who lived at the back of the ridge. If anyone were to be tongue-tied, she should think it would be him. After all, she had three degrees and he hadn't even finished high school. But that aside, his touch sent shivers up her arm, leaving behind a delicious warmth.

"Dr. Allen?"

Josie took a step back. She must get hold of herself. Her behavior was perfectly ridiculous. "I'm sorry, Cole. It's been a long morning. So far, anything that could go wrong has."

He frowned. "Sorry to hear that."

From his expression and tone, she could see that he truly was sorry that she was having a bad day. She shrugged and said, "Happens to everyone from time to time. Were you able to repair the pipe?"

He wiped his hands with a red rag and nodded. "Pretty much did everything I could out here, but I'd like to have a look inside."

"Certainly," she replied, and then led him to the back door. She pulled her keys from her purse and inserted the correct one into the lock. After several tries with the old skeleton key, the tumblers finally turned. When she pushed the door open, a gush of water rushed out onto the back porch, splashing across her new leather flats. "Oh no!"

Cole grasped her arm and pulled her out of the way of the stream of water running past them, then looked around her into the house. He assessed the situation, removed his work boots and socks, and preceded her into the kitchen. Though dread pulled at her, Josie slipped off her soaked shoes and followed him.

"Well, it's not too bad. Could've been much worse," he said. "Looks like most of the leak was confined to the kitchen area. This won't take long to clean up." He turned to her and said, "You just go on back to work and leave everything to me."

There was something very intimate about seeing a gorgeous man in well-worn, threadbare jeans and a form fitting t-shirt standing in the middle of her kitchen barefoot. Again, Josie had difficulty forming a coherent sentence for reply.

*This must stop.*

She cleared her throat and focused on the fruit bowl sitting on her kitchen island. "Cole, you've already done more than any reasonable person would expect."

"Just bein' neighborly."

That aside, she didn't want to further inconvenience him. "Cole, I appreciate all that you've done, but —"

"What are you afraid of, *Dr.* Allen?" His easy smile disintegrated into a flat, hard line. "Think I'll steal your valuables?"

"No, of course not!" She was appalled that he'd even think such a thing. She was not prejudiced. She'd grown up watching how people up on the ridge treated everyone who lived on the back side of the ridge like they were beneath them. She'd hated that.

But even as she thought it, she reminded herself that she'd been thinking all morning how much more educated she was than Cole. Her thoughts must have shown through. Ashamed, she didn't like herself very much at the moment. This man deserved nothing less than her respect, and she intended to prove that to him.

"Cole, I realize that up until this point, I've done nothing to indicate that I am not at all like some of the people who live up here. I genuinely do appreciate what you've done for me today, but I wouldn't think to impose on you to clean up this mess. I'm sure you have other things to accomplish today."

He looked away and swallowed what Josie hoped was his irritation with her. Or should she say "her kind?"

When he turned back to her, he said, "I

just wanted to help out. Nothing more, nothing less."

Josie looked into his eyes, and her heart tightened at what she saw. This proud man had spent his entire life helping people. She remembered him showing kindness to her on more than one occasion. But she, like the majority of the people up here, had not treated him as an equal. Josie Allen would no longer be counted among them.

She extended her hand to Cole and said, "Thank you. I appreciate your kindness."

Without hesitation, he took her hand, which had never worked on anything harder than a computer keyboard, and engulfed it with his, that had known nothing but physical labor from the time he was a boy. At that moment, she felt the tenuous thread of an unlikely friendship form.

"I'll lock up when I leave," he softly promised, still holding her hand in his.

Josie nodded and pulled her tingling hand back, then delved into her purse to cover her reaction. "Let me write you a check."

Shaking his head, he clasped her forearm and pulled her hand out of her bag. "Consider it a welcome home gift."

"Oh, but I couldn't —"

He laid a finger against her lips. She blinked, startled by such intimacy, yet intrigued at such openness. He slowly trailed the tip of his finger along the curve of her lip before easing his hands into his pockets. She pressed a hand to her chest, more to make sure her heart didn't race right out of it than anything else.

"Course you can. I insist."

Josie smiled. Everyone knew there was no arguing with a Craig when they refused compensation. She'd just have to think of another way to repay him.

Josie Lee Allen.

Cole watched her walk barefoot down the sidewalk in front of her house carrying her wet shoes as she headed back to town. She'd been pretty as a picture when she was a little girl. Her mama had sent her to school in those frilly dresses with ruffled petticoats and curled her golden red hair into ringlets that fell clear down to her waist. She'd gone through an awkward stage in middle and high school, but she'd come through it real nice.

He sat down on her front steps and gave the memories free rein. Growing up, he was sure she'd been given everything a little girl could ever dream of. She should have been happy, but she'd always seemed more suited to the company of her books than people.

He remembered staring at her as she read, wondering what she found so fascinating in those boring books. So fascinating that she never even gave him, or anyone else, a second glance.

Now that little girl had grown into a woman so beautiful just looking at her made him ache. Even with her hair wrapped up in a tight knot at the back of her head and wearing a shapeless suit, when he'd stood close to her, it had been all he could do to keep his hands to himself.

Josie Lee Allen. God had been smiling down on him today when he'd found that leaky pipe under her house. He'd been looking for an excuse to speak to her since he'd seen her sitting on the park bench under the old oak tree in Town Square a week ago. She'd been eating an apple and reading a book. The scene rocketed him back about ten years.

He'd been painting the gazebo that stood in the middle of town. She'd been sitting on that same park bench reading. He kept stealing glances at her, wondering what she was reading. She'd worn that gorgeous red hair in a ponytail back then. Her drab sweatshirt and long skirt weren't becoming, but there was something about her that intrigued him.

About that time, some preppy rich boys who'd been tossing a football around called out, "Hey Coal Bucket, I think you have more paint on you than that wood."

Cole ignored them, even when they said something about him being *dumb* as a coal bucket. Real original. But when they turned their attention to Josie, that was another matter. He put down his paint brush when they called her curly red hair a rat's nest.

"She's got mice livin' in there."

"Yeah. They're her pets. Wonder what their names are?"

"Leave her alone," Cole warned.

"What are you going to do about it?" one of the boys asked.

Cole took one menacing step toward them, and they ran like he'd figured. The surprise came when Josie stretched out a leg and sent one of them sprawling face first into the brown mud.

"Now who looks like a coal bucket," she commented with an innocent smile.

He'd known right then and there — Josie Allen was a mystery he wanted to solve.

Still wanted to solve. Which was why he'd cleared his busy schedule and made sure he could be in town for the next couple of weeks, hoping to find an opportunity to talk to her. He'd seen her out a couple of times in the past week, but she'd always been in a hurry with her mind too focused on other things to notice him. Not much had changed there.

He'd even gone into the library to check out a few books hoping to catch a glimpse of her, but her office was way in the back of the huge old building, and she hardly ever came out of it. In fact, from what he could tell, she practically lived there. By the time he got to Miss Estelee's on Monday and Thursday mornings to mow or take care of whatever needed tendin', Josie was already gone. Most nights, when he drove by the library on his way home, all the lights would be out except for the one on the ground floor in the back of the building that had to be her office.

Sighing, Cole stood and sauntered around Josie's house to the back door and into the soggy kitchen. He found a mop in the pantry and got to work.

Yep, Miss Estelee's angels had finally smiled down on him today, because she'd seen him. Really seen him.

Standing here in the kitchen of her fancy house on the ridge, she'd looked into his eyes. She hadn't looked down her nose at him like most folks up here did either. She'd shown him respect. And dare he hope?

Something more. Maybe friendship.

That wasn't anywhere near what he had in mind, but it was a start.

# CHAPTER 2

"Josephine! There you are."

Josie looked up from her work to find an exasperated Martin McKay hurrying into her office. Her secretary, Teresa, stood in the doorway shaking her head in apology.

Josie waved her away and said, "Hello, Martin."

The diminutive man walked around her desk, took her hands, and kissed both her cheeks with affected charm. She tried not to wince. The kiss left a disgusting moistness on her face she longed to wipe away.

Martin, who had an MBA from Harvard — and made sure everyone knew it — had recently taken over running the bank from his father. The McKays had owned the bank and endowed the library for more than a century. They'd also financed her graduate education. A decision she'd already lived to regret.

"I've been looking everywhere for you."

Josie pulled her hands from his and removed her glasses. "I've been right here all day." She didn't know where else he'd expect her to be during business hours. But that was Martin. His head was so filled with learning, there seemed little room for the practical.

"I've managed to secure box seats at the opera this weekend. The Knoxville Opera Company will be performing *Aïda*. We have so little opportunity to partake of the fine arts in our little hamlet, I knew you'd be dying for a bit of culture."

Somewhere in that dissertation, Josie felt certain, there lurked an invitation. She'd been to dinner with Martin once since she'd returned to Angel Ridge. A long, tedious affair filled with endless information centering on the McKays and Martin. A long drive into Knoxville, which would surely include another of these dinners, and then the performance, and the return drive? She wasn't sure she could endure it.

"It sounds wonderful, Martin, but I have so much work to do before I can get my new electronic cataloging system up and running. You know I'm expected to have it and the new website operational by the town's Memorial Day celebration in two weeks."

"Yes, yes. Mother told me. She's all a-twitter over our little country library having the most sophisticated cataloging system in the nation."

"It will be quite a coup, thanks to your family's generosity, of course."

Martin frowned and screwed up his mouth in a very unappealing manner. Being an only child, he'd never become accustomed to the negative response. "You simply must come, Josephine. Who else would go with me on such short notice? You're practically the only suitable person in town for me to invite."

*Suitable. How charming. And he knows I can't turn him down.* Of course, only persons of "suitable" social status would be afforded an invitation by the only son and heir of Angel Ridge's most prominent — and affluent — family.

"I'm sorry to disappoint you, Martin," Josie lied, "but I'm afraid I must give this cataloging program my complete attention. Memorial Day is only a few weeks away, and I simply can't disappoint your mother." She wasn't about to tip him off that the program was not working properly.

"No, of course you can't," he whined. "Why don't you hire someone to help you?"

"I'm afraid there are no funds for that, at

present." She'd begged the board for new computers. They'd felt the extravagant purchase unnecessary since they'd just installed new computers less than ten years ago. Arguing had proved to be a wasted effort. "It will be quicker this way, since this is my program. You know, I created it as part of my doctoral dissertation —"

"What shall I do," he interrupted, "if you do not consent to accompany me?"

"Why don't you offer the tickets to your parents? I'm sure they'd enjoy an evening at the opera."

"Perhaps."

Poor fellow. He looked like he'd dropped his ice cream in the dirt. She couldn't help smiling at the image. His mother had probably never allowed him something as simple as an ice cream from a street vendor. "I am sorry, Martin." And she was. Sorry that he was so spoiled. Sorry that he'd been so isolated as a child by his family that he had no friends. Had no idea how to relate to "common" people.

Isolation seemed the one thing that she and Martin shared. She'd always preferred her books to relationships. For an only child, they were pure entertainment. They made no demands. Had no expectations and did not disappoint. The worlds she read about were always places where she'd fit in.

"Well," Martin waved his hand at Josie's computer, "if you get the bugs worked out of that thing before week's end, let me know."

"I'll do that."

After Martin left, Josie grabbed a tissue and scrubbed her cheeks. She rested her head back against her chair, suddenly feeling exhausted. How she longed for a break. But the town's expectations weighed on her — had weighed on her most of her life.

She'd heard it often enough in school. Her teachers had singled her out. Separated her from her peers. So intelligent, so gifted. Her mother had always told her, *To whom much is given, much is expected.* Everyone in Angel Ridge seemed to demand better than her best. And now their demands focused on her responsibilities toward their prestigious library.

Sitting at the end of Main, it was an enormous, three-story brick structure built in the style of a medieval castle. Like a castle, it had always been a magical place for Josie.

Now, she saw the library as an adult who'd spent the last seven years of her life learning to run a library. She saw things in a more realistic light. Maybe too realistic. The library was big because the McKays didn't do anything on a small scale. It was also big out of necessity. The library was more than just a place to check out books and do research. It housed special collections of the Tennessee presidents' papers and artifacts, Tennessee historical documents and maps, the largest genealogical collection in the state. It even boasted an art gallery that included the McKay Collection as well as traveling exhibits.

Since she'd taken over, things hadn't turned out at all like she'd planned. Mrs. McKay had been on her back non-stop. Martin was bent on pursuing her. The program wasn't working. Nothing was going right.

Josie pinched the bridge of her nose. She was so tired. She'd come home and taken this job with hardly a break anywhere along the way. Now, still more was expected of her. She had to make operational the most innovative cataloging system in the industry.

No problem. She could do it. She must do it. It was expected.

But she'd give anything for a few hours in the company of a person who had no pre-conceived notions of Josephine Allen. Her books held no expectations, no lofty aspirations. They didn't care how she looked or how she conducted herself — but what a lonely existence they provided.

She was nearly twenty-six and had never had a real relationship. Dates. She wondered what normal dates were like. In high school, no one had asked her out. In college, she'd never had the time to date like the other girls. Making straight A's required giving her studies her complete attention. But now that her studies were at an end —

"Five o'clock, Dr. Allen. I'm outta here."

Josie turned to her secretary. "Thanks, Teresa. Would you please ask Mildred to shoo the people out of genealogy and lock up on her way out?"

"Sure thing. You working late again?"

"I'm afraid so. I have to iron out these problems with the program."

"Maybe you just need to get away from it for awhile. Get out, have some dinner, catch a movie. You know, do something mindless, then come back tomorrow with a new perspective."

Josie smiled. It always amazed her what conventional wisdom Teresa offered. She made it all seem so simple . . . and tempting. "Thanks, Teresa. You know, I just might do that."

Teresa smiled. "See you tomorrow."

But first, she had to try one more thing

39

with the program. . . .

Josie heard something — or someone — tapping on the window of her office and nearly jumped out of her skin. She grabbed a letter opener and backed away from the window, edging around the corner of her desk to where the phone sat. Picking up the receiver, she started dialing 911.

"Josie — it's me, Cole."

"Cole?" Josie peered through the hundred-year-old leaded glass panes into the darkness and saw that, indeed, he was standing outside her window. She glanced at her watch. Nearly nine o'clock! She must have lost track of time. Again.

She hung up the phone and walked over to the double window. She grasped the handle and pushed one side open. "Cole — what are you doing here?"

"What are you doing at work this late?" he countered. "It's not safe for a lady to be out walkin' the streets alone this time of night."

Josie laughed. "The crime rate in Angel Ridge is almost nil. Besides, the Constable usually keeps an eye on me as I walk home. It isn't far."

"Don't look now, but Henry's snoozin' down by the angel monument."

40

The uniformed man was propped up against the brick pedestal of the monument with his hat tipped down over his eyes. She laughed again.

The vertically long window was only a few feet above the ground, so Cole gracefully swung his more than six foot frame through the opening, then sat, slinging one foot inside and propping the other on the wide pink marble sill. Josie's breath hung in her throat. He wore faded jeans that fit his muscular legs to perfection. A black t-shirt stretched taut against impossibly wide shoulders. The dark color contrasted nicely with his pale hair. He'd pulled it back in a ponytail. She felt more than a little disappointed. She liked it down.

"Tell me, what goes on in a library to keep a person here to all hours of the night?" he was saying.

Josie sat back down and stared at him. She'd never encountered a man so elementally rugged. The men of her experience were scholarly, professor types. Men at home in a library. Men with soft hands and pale skin. Men who pursued academia. But here she sat, in her element, and Cole Craig had climbed into her domain through the window. She couldn't hold back her smile. He seemed right at home. Correction. Sexy and right at home.

"I've been working on a new cataloging system. It's a program I developed myself. It worked fine in the clinical trials I put it through, but now that I'm trying to implement the system, I'm finding problems."

"How long you been workin' on it?"

He was rubbing his hand from his knee to his thigh and back again in a slow motion Josie found mesmerizing. She shook her head. What had he asked? Oh. The program. How long she'd been working on it.

"*Um,* all day — every day — since I got back." She shifted her focus from his tantalizing thighs to the computer screen and frowned. "It worked fine when I defended my dissertation. But now —" She rolled the mouse and the stupid computer froze again. She closed her eyes and sighed.

"What's it supposed to do?"

"When working properly, it should catalog the library's holdings and make accessible its entire collection via the Internet. The system supports instant messaging with staff members who can provide information from any book in the library." Her words rushed out, reflecting the enthusiasm she'd first felt when developing her program. "All the genealogy materials would be accessible online. It even provides virtual tours of the special collections on a special area of the website."

And it was up to her to get all this running on these dinosauric computers, beginning with converting the ancient card catalog to an electronic system. Surely they were the last library in the country to still use one.

"I'm sorry." She turned her attention back to Cole who sat watching her avidly. "I'm sure you're not interested in this much detail."

"Sounds fascinating," he said with a slow grin. "But maybe you need to get away from it for awhile."

She rubbed her forehead, willing the dull ache there to go away. "That seems to be the consensus."

"The blue plate dinner special down at Ferguson's is chicken and dumplings with corn muffins."

At the mention of food, Josie's stomach growled. She'd skipped lunch to go home.

Cole grinned. He must have heard the loud rumbling.

"Have you eaten today?"

Now that she thought about it, she'd skipped breakfast as well because she'd almost been late to work. She shrugged. "I guess I forgot."

He stood. "Well, no wonder you can't think straight. How do you expect to be sharp when you've got no nourishment in your system?" He shut and locked the window.

Practicalities. Hadn't she just accused Martin of having no mind for the practical? "I've been so busy, I just —"

He reached across her desk, deftly unlocked the computer, saved her work, and shut it down. Josie barely had time to be surprised that he even knew where the power button was, let alone the way he forced her decision, before he said, "Let's go."

She grabbed her purse as he took her arm and hustled her out of the office. "Where are we going?"

"To Ferguson's. You know, food? You've not eaten."

Yeah. She was following. Following Cole Craig through the deserted, darkened library to the front door. Full-blown fantasies of the two of them taking a detour into the stacks bloomed in her mind. She shook her head. Cole. The front door.

Josie switched off the lights, hesitating. She had to eat, but with Cole? What would people think? More specifically, what would Mrs. McKay say? Would she use it as another excuse to remind Josie she'd paid for her graduate education? Probably.

After a moment's thought, she said, "It's late. I should just go home and microwave something."

"Not tonight. You owe me dinner for all that work I put in at your place today, and I've got a hankerin' for Dixie's chicken and dumplings."

He opened the front door for her, and she walked out in front of him. She scanned the streets to make sure no one saw them, then his words hit her. The leaky pipe! Good grief, she'd forgotten all about it. She turned to lock the door. "I'm sorry, Cole. I've been so self-absorbed, I didn't even ask. Did everything go all right at my house? Did the clean-up take long?"

As they walked down the sidewalk toward the diner, he took her hand and placed it in the bend of his arm before he shoved his hands into his pockets. "If I say it wasn't too bad, are you gonna go home and leave me to eat alone?"

Looking up into his handsome face illuminated by the dim light of the street lamps, she found him completely irresistible. His arm felt hard and muscled, warm and very real beneath her hand. Infinitely more appealing than paper and computer keyboards. "I suppose the least I can do is buy you supper for all your trouble."

He threw back his shoulders, puffed out his chest and said, "Well now, I'd have to agree. I've saved you from a disaster at home and near starvation all in one day. Why, I'm like a bonafide knight ridin' to your rescue."

She smacked his rock hard stomach with the back of her hand, and he doubled over in affected pain. "Don't get too cocky. Now if you could cure my computer problems . . ."

"We'll work on that tomorrow."

Josie laughed. "Deal," she said, but didn't give an ounce of credence to the notion that Cole Craig could iron out the kinks in a complicated computer program. He might be able to work wonders with an antiquated plumbing system, but computer programs? Not likely.

They walked down Main on the old brick sidewalk she remembered from her childhood. The town still maintained the antique gas street lamps that gave everything a cozy, intimate glow. Electric streetlights would be more practical, but they wouldn't shimmer across the golden highlights in Cole's hair like a lover's caress.

"What're you thinkin'?"

"That the town hasn't changed much."

"Depends on what you call change. There's a new beauty parlor openin' up across from the bank." He leaned down so he could whisper close to her ear. "I hear tell they're gonna sell fancy lingerie there, too."

Josie laughed, more to cover her nervousness than anything else. "That ought to get Mrs. McKay worked up."

A lazy smile transformed Cole's face, and Josie found simply breathing a bit difficult.

"That lady wouldn't know what to do with herself if she didn't have somethin' to get worked up about."

But if the old biddy had that distraction, maybe she wouldn't be on Josie's back twenty-four/seven. Just the thought lifted her spirits.

Most of the brick buildings lining the street were decorated with scalloped red, white, and blue banners in anticipation of the town Memorial Day celebration. Both the Baptist and the Presbyterian churches at the end of Main proudly flew the American and Christian flags. In less than two weeks, the street would be filled with vendors selling mouth-watering foods and homemade crafts. In less than two weeks, she was expected to debut her computer program.

"What's wrong?" Cole asked.

They stood in front of Wallace's Apothecary. She hadn't been aware that she'd stopped moving. "Oh. I was just thinking about work."

"None of that, now. You need a break."

"But —"

He clasped her hand and pulled her along. "You promised me dinner. That computer will be there in the mornin', I promise."

At the end of the street, they turned left into the front door of Ferguson's. The bell clanged announcing their arrival as Cole held it open for Josie to pass through. The diner was practically deserted at this late hour. Good. He wanted her all to himself. He didn't mind not having to deal with speculative glances and people gossiping about why the town librarian was out with Angel Ridge's finest handyman. Not tonight.

"Hey, Cole." Dixie called out from behind the counter.

Cole smiled at the tall woman who'd styled her short, red-tinted black hair into a spiked, punk look. "Hey, Dix."

"As I live and breathe, if it ain't Josie Allen. Or should I call you Dr. Allen now?"

"Josie's fine."

"Good to see ya. Sit wherever you want. I'll be with you in a sec."

He stopped at a booth near a window. "This okay?"

"How about over here?"

She pointed to a booth against a back wall that was more out of the way. Cole shrugged and followed her. He'd never turn down the opportunity to share a corner booth with Josie Allen. Not in this lifetime.

Cole watched with interest as Josie unbuttoned her blazer and slid across the smooth green upholstered seat of the booth. The quick movement only provided a brief glimpse of a conservative, pale blue blouse before she pulled the material of the jacket together. Maybe she'd take it off later. . . .

The light green linoleum of the table was accented by a small vase with a single, white daisy. As usual, the place was spotless.

"I haven't eaten here in years."

He had to work at focusing on anything but her. "Then you're in for a treat. Dixie's food just gets better with time."

"I heard that." Dixie slapped Cole on the shoulder with her order pad. "Everything served here is fresh."

"*Ow.*" He rubbed his shoulder. "You know what I mean, Dix."

"*Uh-huh.* What can I get you folks?"

"We'll have the special with sweet tea."

Dixie looked at Josie for approval.

"Sounds good," she agreed.

"Nice apron, Dix," Cole said.

Dixie, who was known for her unusual outfits, wore a bright neon green sleeveless dress with vibrant pink polka dots. Her apron was the reverse. Pink with green polka dots. Anyone else would have looked like a clown, but Dixie pulled it off.

"You here to critique my wardrobe or are you hungry?"

"I'm here to eat."

Dixie nodded. "Two teas and two specials. Comin' right up. And welcome home, Josie. It's good to see you around this old town again."

"I'll second that," Cole said.

"Thanks," she said to both.

"So, how many years has it been?" he asked.

"Well, I've been away at school for seven years, but it's been longer than that since I saw you."

A particularly vivid memory came to mind. "It's not been that long."

Josie frowned. "What do you mean?"

"There was one Christmas you came home from college. I saw you at Christmas Eve services with your folks."

"Really?"

"You were wearing a black dress and your hair hung loose around your shoulders. You looked beautiful."

She tipped her head to the side and gave him a sheepish look. "I talked my parents into having Christmas here that year. I hated Christmases in Florida at their condo. For some reason, I was incredibly homesick that year. For the town and the library, anyway. I never had any real friends here."

"That why you never visited during breaks?"

She unrolled her silverware and smoothed her napkin in her lap. "I don't remember seeing you at services that year."

He didn't miss that she had neatly avoided answering his question, but he let it go. "It was pretty crowded."

She nodded. "Always is."

That had been the first time he'd noticed her. Really noticed her . . . as a woman. That little black dress had hugged her body in all the right places and her thick long hair had spilled down her back and over the pew. If he'd died on the spot, he'd have gone straight to hell because he'd fantasized about seein' it spread out on his pillow. . . .

He blinked and brought his thoughts back to the present. Petite and thin, that boxy suit she wore today hid any shape that might lie beneath it. But he could imagine. She still had that flame red hair. Wonder if it still reached her waist?

Looking at Cole now, Josie couldn't imagine overlooking a man as handsome and magnetic as Cole even in a crowd. She tried to remember the last time she saw him. "You know, I came home for a whole summer after I graduated from college. I don't think I saw you once in the nearly three months I was here."

The vinyl creaked as he shifted his position on the seat of the booth. He looked uncomfortable. Cole lowered his head, but not before she saw a crimson blush stain his high cheekbones. He must be embarrassed by the fact that he had to drop out of school when she had gone on to explore all that higher education had to offer. She wanted to put him at ease, but she couldn't resist reminding him of that time in middle school.

"I seem to recall you defending my honor on the playground. Remember? I was in sixth grade. You were in eighth, I think. The kids were always teasing me about reading during recess instead of playing."

"I remember."

"That day, Bobby Jones was throwing

rocks at me. One hit my leg and made it bleed."

"Jones had a mean streak in him a mile wide."

Josie nodded. "You took him aside and said something to him."

"I couldn't understand why anyone would want to read instead of play, but I figured if that was what you wanted to do, you oughta be able to do it in peace."

"He never bothered me again after that, thanks to you. I always wondered what you said to him."

The color in his cheeks deepened. "That was a long time ago, Josie."

"Bobby seemed to take particular pleasure in making me miserable. I just wanted to let you know how much it meant, you taking up for me the way you did."

"It was nothin'."

"I figured he would start torturing me again after you left for high school, but he didn't."

He looked even more uncomfortable. He turned and stared out the window, then glanced over his shoulder toward the front counter. "Wonder where Dixie is with that tea?"

On impulse, she reached out and touched the back of his hand. "Why did Bobby leave me alone after that day?"

His sigh was heavy with resignation. He turned his hand over and rubbed his thumb against the back of her wrist. "Because I made sure he wouldn't bother you again."

His touch was hypnotic. Addictive. "How? You weren't always around to keep an eye on him."

"I let him know that if he did, I'd hear about it and see to it that he'd regret it."

"Oh, Cole. You didn't hit him, did you?"

"Naw. But he knew I would."

Much as she liked the feel of his talented fingers on her wrist, she folded her hands in her lap. "I just wanted to say, you standing up for me, well, it was the nicest thing anyone ever did for me at school."

"It was nothin'," he repeated.

She wished she could make him see what a big deal it had been for her. Her life had changed after that day. So many of the kids had been cruel to her, especially at recess. She always got picked last. Even when she did try to play kickball or whatever game it happened to be, she never was allowed to play. The kids didn't let her touch the ball, and they'd skip her when her turn came around.

So, she'd quit playing. None of the teachers minded. They pretty much let her do what she wanted, because she was a good student. Special. The kids had hated that even more than having to put up with her on their teams. So, they turned their attention to making her as miserable as possible. Until Cole had stood up for her. Still, she could see that no matter what she said, Cole would downplay it. It was his way.

"What have you been doing all these years?"

He played with his silverware. "This and that. Nothing nearly as interesting as you, I'm sure. What kept you away from home all those years?"

"There wasn't much to come back to here. After I left for college, Mom and Dad bought the condo in Florida, and over the years, they spent more and more time there. So, I worked summers at the UNC library. Then during graduate school, I taught classes at Syracuse's Summer Information Science Institute in New York."

He rubbed his jaw. The stubble lining it made him look incredibly sexy and a little dangerous. "Sounds . . ."

"Boring?"

"I was going to say prestigious."

That comment caught her off guard. "Thank you."

"So with your folks gone for good now,

why'd you come back? I'm guessin' you could have gotten a job most anywhere you wanted."

"Being the director of the Angel Ridge Library was always my dream." That much was true. She wouldn't go into the part about the deal she'd brokered with Mrs. McKay that left her with no other choice but to return.

She'd achieved a full academic scholarship from the University of North Carolina at Chapel Hill, finished at the top of her class with a bachelor's degree in library science. Against the odds, she'd been accepted to The University of Illinois Urbana-Champaign, the top graduate program in the country for information science. But because of a couple of *C*'s in math, she'd been passed over for a graduate assistantship in favor of candidates with 4.0's.

That summer, she'd come home and worked part-time here in the library. She'd have given anything to be the director of such a prestigious library, but Josie knew her dream would slip from her grasp if she couldn't find the money for graduate school. Mrs. McKay would never allow someone who only had a B.S. to run the place.

When Mrs. McKay sat her down and offered to finance her graduate education if she committed to taking over for old Mrs. White when she retired, Josie couldn't believe it. She hadn't given the decision any thought.

"Well, I know everybody's glad you did," Cole drawled, drawing her attention back to their conversation. "You're about all this town's talked about for years. And now that you're back —"

"Please," Josie held up a hand. She couldn't take another minute of what great things the town expected of her. Reaching back, she pulled the pins from her hair. "Let's don't talk about that, okay?" She shook her hair out and rubbed her scalp. It felt good to let the weight of it fall loose around her shoulders.

"Sure."

Josie met Cole's eyes. Stunned was the only adequate word to describe his expression. She opened her mouth to ask what was the matter when Dixie returned with their drinks.

"You look like you need some fattening up, Josie Lee," she commented as she set big glasses of iced tea in front of them and a plate full of lemon quarters. "You know, I still make those chicken salad sandwiches you used to love."

"I'll have to make a point to pull myself

away from work and come over for lunch."

"That place sure is keepin' you busy." She shook her head. "Well, if you can't come by, just call. I'll have Blake run one over to you. Like most of the town, he's usually around at lunchtime."

"What's that brother of yours into these days?" Cole asked. "Haven't seen him in awhile."

"He's contributing to suburban sprawl. You know, takin' somebody's farmland and turnin' it into a subdivision."

Cole chuckled. "It pays the bills."

"It oughta be a crime," Dixie said in that matter-of-fact way of hers, laced with the remnants of a Texan accent. "Those dumplings are comin' right up," she said over her shoulder as she hurried away.

"Good to see some things haven't changed. You can always count on Dixie for a definite opinion."

"I heard that!" Dixie called from the kitchen.

Josie and Cole both laughed.

"How's it feel to be back after all these years?"

Josie tucked her hair behind her ears. "In some ways, it's like I never left. Not much has changed."

"People change. I bet you've changed a lot."

Josie thought for a minute. "Not really." She'd grown older, matured from the eighteen-year-old she'd been when she left. She'd accumulated a lot of knowledge, but typically, she hadn't experienced much outside her books.

"Your glasses are gone."

Another comment she hadn't expected. She sipped her tea. "I had corrective surgery a couple of years ago. Now I just wear computer glasses. They're mainly to alleviate eyestrain."

Cole's gaze swept her face. "I never noticed how beautiful your eyes are."

Josie rearranged the silverware on her napkin. "How could you? My glasses were so thick."

"I'm noticing now. They remind me of warm honey."

His husky tone ran through her veins like choice brandy.

Josie laughed nervously. "I think you're just hungry."

Their food arrived, diffusing the sensually charged moment. They turned their attention to the delicious meal. "*Mmm . . .* I'd forgotten what good home cooking tasted like."

"I'm sure you do just as well," Cole said.

"Oh, no. I never learned how to cook. If it weren't for the microwave, prepared frozen meals, and peanut butter, I'm afraid I'd starve."

"Well, I'll have to see to it that you eat out more often."

There it was. He would ask her out again. She should tell him there wouldn't be a next time, but she couldn't deny that she was tempted to throw convention to the wind . . . maybe even experience a real date. Cole was so different from the men of her narrow experience.

But resisting temptation, she said, "I stay pretty busy."

"Bein' as I'm your unofficial knight, I feel it's my duty to save you from nuked frozen dinners."

Josie giggled. She couldn't help herself. She sat back and stared at him. He was certainly easy on the eyes. The light above the booth made his hair shine like spun gold and highlighted the brilliant blue of his eyes. She could look at him all night. "It's late," she said instead. "I should be going."

Cole wiped his mouth on his napkin. "I'll walk with you." He slid out of the booth and held out his hand to help her up.

She put her hand in his. "That's okay. I

can see myself home."

He looked taken aback. "I wouldn't dream of letting you walk all that way alone at this time of night. So, don't think to try and talk me out of it."

"He means it, too." Dixie dipped her chin and wagged a finger with a polished pink fingernail at her. "You might as well not argue."

Josie reached for her purse. "You didn't give us a ticket, Dixie."

"It's on me. Call it a welcome home meal. Here's you some apple pie for a midnight snack." She winked at Josie, then looked at Cole. "Hot and fresh."

She handed Josie the paper bag. Dixie's double meaning wasn't missed on Josie. The wonderful smell of cinnamon and apples wafted up to tease her senses. "Thanks, Dixie. I appreciate that."

"Don't mention it. Ya'll have a nice evenin' now, hear?"

There was that wink again. Josie suppressed a groan. This would be all over town tomorrow.

Cole escorted Josie to the door and out onto the sidewalk. It was a perfect springtime Angel Ridge evening. She inhaled deeply. A hint of roses wafted on the breeze. These pleasant evenings would soon turn to summer and hot steamy nights. That thought conjured another hot image. Josie shook her head. What was wrong with her?

"Nice night," Cole commented, his voice soft and low, as they walked toward the residential end of town.

"Yes." She tipped her head up to the sky. "Have you ever seen so many stars?"

"Beautiful," he agreed as they turned off Main Street onto Ridge Road, but with him looking at her instead of up at the sky, Josie knew he wasn't referring to the stars.

She smiled at the simple compliment, unused to this kind of attention. Most people complimented her mind, not her looks. She kept her focus on the sky. "I missed this while I was away. The stars here seem closer. Brighter."

"There aren't any street lights. It makes a difference."

"I guess you're right," she agreed, looking around. "Only a few porch lights and lampposts."

"I love these old houses up here. Did you know Miss Estelee's is the oldest?"

"No."

"She's not sure exactly when it was built, but best I can tell, it was probably in the early 1800s."

"Really?"

He nodded. "At first glance, it's a standard *I* design like you see in most farmhouses, but on a much smaller scale. The really interesting thing is the butterfly plan that gives the front that unusual *V* shape with the two wings jutting out at either side of the front porch capped by those nice bay windows. Very different from all these Victorians."

"I guess I never thought about it."

"Well, over the years, they doctored it up with Victorian elements, like the gingerbread trim up in the eaves and on the porch posts."

"Now I did notice the trim. There are angel's wings in it."

"No surprise there."

When they reached the gate in the picket fence in front of her house, she said, "Here we are."

Cole released the latch on the gate and held it open for her.

"I can manage from here," she said.

"I'll walk you to the door. Make sure your key works. Those skeleton locks in these old houses can be persnickety."

She smiled and preceded him up the sidewalk.

"Howdy-do!"

Josie stopped on the first step leading up to her front porch. She peered into the darkness toward her neighbor's house. "Miss Estelee?"

"Howdy-do, Josie," she said.

"Is everything all right?"

"Right as rain. The cold's kept me cooped up so long, I missed lookin' at the stars, so I thought I'd rock a spell." Her old chair creaked with the motion. "You workin' late again?"

"Yes, ma'am."

"Who's that with you there?"

"It's me, Miss Estelee. Cole Craig."

"Oh, howdy-do, Cole. You still fixin' things for Josie?"

"Uh, no. Just seein' she gets home safe."

"That's a nice boy. She needs tendin'. Well, gittin' late. Time for an old lady to be in bed." The squeak of her rocking chair stopped as she rose slowly to her feet. Her silver-blue hair glinted in the moonlight as she peered over the porch railing at them.

"Is there anything I can do for you, ma'am?" Cole asked.

"Oh, no. You two young'uns enjoy your evenin' now, hear?"

"Good night, Miss Estelee," Josie said.

"Night . . ." her voice trailed off. The bang of a screen door announced that she'd retreated into the house. Josie wondered what Miss Estelee would read into Cole

Craig "seein' her home." People shouldn't get the wrong idea. She regretted the thought almost immediately. Why did she care what people thought? Just because most people on the Ridge thought that way didn't mean she had to.

She retrieved the keys from her purse and unlocked the door. Luckily, the lock wasn't temperamental tonight. She opened the door and reached inside to turn on the foyer light. Josie leaned against the doorframe, not inviting Cole in. She held the bag containing Dixie's apple pie between them like a buffer.

"So, what are you doin' tomorrow?" he asked.

"Working. What else is there?"

"You know," he trailed a finger down her cheek, "there's a whole world outside books just waitin' for you to explore it."

Her cheek tingled where he'd touched her. She liked the feeling. Explore the world. For the first time in her life, she'd been thinking the exact same thing, but she wouldn't admit it. Thoughts like that led to distractions she couldn't afford. Not now.

"Maybe I'll get to that some day." Her voice sounded weak.

Where was her resolve? All she could think was that it wouldn't take much for him to lean down and kiss her. In fact, the way he focused on her mouth seemed to indicate that was just what he intended. If he did, she had a feeling it wouldn't be nearly as disgusting as when Martin had kissed her. Cole's kiss would be unlike anything she'd ever experienced.

Cole rested a hand on the doorframe near her head bringing his tempting body even closer to hers. "After you deal with your problems at the library?"

Problems at the library? She nearly missed his meaning when all she could think about was what it would be like if he did kiss her. "Yes . . . library . . . problems . . . yes."

He smoothed the backs of his fingers from her cheek down to her chin. "You'll work it out, Josie. I have no doubt."

Mesmerizing. He had the most mesmerizing eyes.

"And when you do, I'll expect you to take me to dinner. Since you didn't have to buy tonight, you still owe me."

*"Mmm."* She moistened suddenly dry lips with the tip of her tongue.

Finally, he leaned down and kissed her on the cheek. A too brief caress that ended almost as soon as it began. "Goodnight, Josie Lee."

She watched him turn and walk away.

Disappointment left a hollow feeling inside her. She shifted from one foot to the other. She didn't want him to go, but she knew he should before she lost all sense of any kind of resolve she might have a tenuous grip on. Still, she called out, "Cole?"

He stopped on the bottom step and looked back up at her. Silhouetted in the glow of her porch light, he looked like an angel come down to earth.

She held out the bag of pie. "Why don't you take this?"

"You keep it. For those nights when you forget to eat supper."

She nodded. "Thank you. I appreciate all you did for me today."

He flashed an easy smile and said, "Anytime."

Alone on her porch, Josie touched her fingers to her cheek. She'd been right. Cole's kiss was nothing like Martin's.

Sleep was a long time in coming that night. Every time she closed her eyes, instead of trying to work out the problem with her cataloging program in her head, all she could see was Cole Craig's face so close to hers. She remembered the warmth of his body brushing against hers as he leaned in to kiss her. In her fantasy, it wasn't a chaste kiss on the cheek.

He'd pull her up against his chest and with a hand in her hair, he'd touch his lips to hers. . . .

At last, she cupped her hand against the cheek his lips had caressed and faded off to sleep.

# CHAPTER 3

"Mornin', Dix."

Cole slid onto a stool at the counter of Ferguson's Diner. The lunch rush was just coming in to take advantage of the daily special despite the fact that some still lingered over their morning coffee.

Dixie turned with a steaming pot of coffee in her hand. "What happened to you? You look like ten miles of bad road." She set a cup in front of him and poured.

The clattering hurt his aching head. "Nice to see you, too." He scanned the room. "Is it more crowded than usual in here?"

"About three or four van loads of seniors are spendin' the day up at the library. Researchin' their family history, combin' through the special collections, you know. Typical stuff around here now that the weather's turned nice."

Cole nodded. He'd know that if he was around more. Mention of the library brought Josie to mind. He ought to go up and see her. He scrubbed a hand across the stubble covering his chin. He really should have shaved, but he'd been so tired when he got up, he'd been afraid of slicing his throat if he'd attempted it. Maybe he'd go by after he'd had a chance to go home and clean up.

Dixie just smiled and plopped an order pad on the counter in front of him. "So, it went well with Josie last night?"

Cole frowned. He couldn't say how it had gone. To say the town librarian was sending mixed signals would be a gross understatement.

Dixie crossed her arms and leaned a hip against the counter in front of him. "Must have gone real well, judging by the looks of you." She wiggled her eyebrows. "Guess you didn't make it home last night."

He felt heat climb up his throat to his cheeks. He looked from left to right to make sure no one was listening to their conversation. "You got a dirty mind, Dix. I saw her home. That's all."

"Really?" Skepticism laced her words.

"Yeah. Gimme a break. She just . . . We just —"

"So what kept you up all night, if not . . . that?"

"I just didn't get much sleep."

"I'd say that's pretty clear. Which brings us back to the original question. What kept you up?"

Thoughts of Josie and a project deadline, but he wouldn't admit either to Dixie. She'd just lecture. They'd known each other since they were kids. Hell, her brother Blake and he had been pretty good friends once. They were both too busy these days to get together much anymore. He couldn't remember the last time they'd shared a beer and a game of darts at Heart's Pool Hall.

But even though Dixie usually gave pretty good advice, he wasn't ready to spill his guts about his interest in Josie or anything else. Not to Dixie or anyone.

"You know, just restless I guess."

*"Mmm-hmm."* She leveled him a look that saw right to the heart of the matter. "I'd say something or *someone* has got you all in a dither." She laughed. "I never thought I'd see the day. Who'd have thought it'd take a woman with a Ph.D. to whip Cole Craig."

He glanced around again. "Could you keep your voice down?"

Ignoring that, she asked, "So, what's your plan?"

Cole sipped his coffee. He winced as the hot liquid scorched his throat. "Plan?"

"For wooing Josie."

"I'm flyin' by the seat of my pants here, Dix. There's no plan. Hell, I'm just hopin' she don't decide to kick me to the curb."

"We don't have curbs in Angel Ridge. City ordinance against it."

"You know what I mean."

Dixie leaned in close and spoke in hushed tones. "What are we talking about here, Cole? You just mildly interested in Josie, or is there more to this?"

He hoped his shrug was non-committal.

No dice.

She slapped the counter causing a few heads to turn. Cole closed his eyes and groaned.

" 'Bout time. All right, then. I'm gonna help you out here."

He held his cup up. "Just keep the caffeine comin', would ya?"

Dixie topped him off. "I'll do that and more. If memory serves, Josie's particularly fond of my chicken salad."

"So?"

"*So,*" she intoned, "it's lunchtime."

"It is?" He looked down at his watch and noticed he'd forgotten to put it on. Great.

Dixie jerked a thumb at the clock. It was going on twelve. "Beautiful day for a picnic, wouldn't you say?"

When Cole didn't move or speak, she smacked his shoulder with the back of her hand. He winced, but turned and squinted against the bright sunshine pouring through the front windows of the diner. A picnic.

"You been talkin' to Miss Estelee?"

"No. Why?"

Miss Estelee had said something about a picnic when he'd been trimming her bushes earlier. It's a wonder he remembered anything the woman had said. She'd called him at the crack of dawn, insisting that he trim her boxwoods. She could have mentioned it when he was there yesterday instead of waking him up at an indecent hour insisting that he come to her house first thing.

Dixie snapped her fingers in front of his face. "Hello? Anybody home in there?"

"Sorry. Miss Estelee was saying something earlier about a picnic out by the angel monument. I didn't quite follow." It wasn't unusual for Miss Estelee to go on about things, but this morning, she'd been really worked up, telling him some story about an old love and picnics in the Town Square.

"Sounds like a stellar idea to me. I'll pack some things up. You get yourself awake."

Dixie disappeared into the back. Cole leaned forward and tried to roll some of the kinks out of his neck. A picnic with Josie

73

might be just the thing. She was probably hunched over her computer and wouldn't eat if he didn't take her out. And a picnic in the middle of town would sure test the waters of how she felt about being seen in public with him. Still, was he ready to risk that? Was it too soon?

Dixie dropped a heavy bag in front of him then turned to fill large paper cups with ice and sweet tea.

"I don't know, Dix. What if she says 'no'?" He raked a hand through his hair. He hadn't pulled it back this morning, hadn't shaved. He'd been working outside at Miss Estelee's —

"Life's full of risks. No guts, no glory and all that. Besides, I've never known you to be the kind of man that backs away from a challenge."

She put the cups of tea in a bag and set them next to the other. Cole stared blankly at the food.

Dixie pushed the bags closer to him. "Come on. You're burnin' daylight. Do you want someone else to whisk her away for lunch while you sit here starin' at the food?"

That got his attention. Dixie knew everything about everybody. She must have heard something. "You know somethin' I don't?"

"I heard Martin McKay's been sniffin'

around her. I even heard he took her to some fancy place up in Knoxville for dinner right after she got back in town."

"Come on. Josie Lee and Martin McKay? He's not her type."

Dixie leveled him another one of those looks. "He's exactly her type. Cultured, educated, rich . . ."

"From the right side of town," Cole finished.

"There is that, if that kind of thing concerns you."

His spine stiffened. "Never concerned me before."

She wiped her hands on her apron and said in that matter-of-fact, direct way of hers, "You might want to give it a little thought before you go puttin' your heart on the line. Some folks in town might not take kindly to the two of you seein' each other."

"I never really cared what folks think, either."

"What about Josie?"

"I can't speak for her."

"That about brings us full circle. You gonna sit here and wonder, or you gonna do something about it?"

Cole stood, pulled some bills out of his pocket, and dropped them on the counter.

"Guess I'd best be gettin' over to the library."

Dixie smiled. "Now you're talkin'."

All morning, Josie struggled to keep her mind on her work. However, thoughts of Cole stole her concentration. These feelings she was developing for him surprised her, no doubt about it. Who'd have thought she'd ever go for a man like Cole Craig.

"*Psst.* Josie."

She turned to find Cole peering in her window. Her heart did a funny little flip at the sight of him. Today, he wore a navy t-shirt with his jeans. Dark stubble shadowed his face and his hair swung loose around his shoulders. She decided she liked him like this. He had a wild, untamed look, even though the hint of curl in his hair softened him a bit.

Hurrying over to the cracked window, she pushed it open. "You know, we do have a front door."

He grinned. "Yeah, but that would be too easy. Good thing these boxwoods haven't been trimmed in awhile or else this would be like usin' the front door, what with everybody passin' by this time of day."

"I was about to speak to the maintenance guy about pruning them."

Cole shook his head. "Not a good move. Fred would wind up butchering them. I'd do it for you, but I'm havin' too much fun." His smile was wide and unrepentant.

Josie pushed the window open wider and sat on the sill. "Well, are you coming in?" After another long morning at the computer, she liked the idea of sitting knee to knee with Cole on her window sill and chatting for a bit.

"Nope."

"No?"

"Nope. You're comin' out." He held up a hand and waited for her to take it.

"I couldn't —"

"Sure you can. Just swing your legs over, and I'll lift you down."

"But —"

"No 'buts.' I'm taking you to lunch."

"I'd planned on working through lunch."

"I got Dixie's chicken salad sandwiches. Your favorite."

Josie's stomach grumbled. "That's not playing fair."

"I never played fair in my life. Why should I start now?" He wiggled his fingers. "Come on."

She chewed on her lower lip, considering. He took her hand and gave it a tug. *"Ah!"* She tumbled out of the window, nothing but air separating her from the ground. But Cole caught and pressed her against his solid chest. She flailed until her arms were secure around his neck.

"*Shh.* I got you," he said close to her ear.

He did indeed. She closed her eyes, enjoying the sensations coursing through her body. He had the broadest shoulders and strongest arms. The kind that made a woman feel small and petite, secure and safe. Not that she needed any of those things. But if she did, he'd certainly be the one to —

He set her on her feet and stepped back. Apparently, he'd been totally unaffected by the contact.

"There ya go. I thought we could head out to the Town Square and picnic by the angel monument." He picked up a blanket and a couple of bags that had been partially concealed by an overgrown bush.

"Okay," Josie agreed, but wondered how she would explain re-entering the library when she was supposed to be in her office working.

His smile was nothing short of brilliant. She smiled, too. Past the courthouse with its clock chiming noon, past the First Presbyterian Church, even past the bank, and all the way to the Town Square. Was it her, or was the sun brighter today? The sky bluer? The robin's song more lyrical? Josie frowned. The Town Square, more crowded with people?

"Here we are." Cole spread out a soft, red plaid blanket on the grassy spot behind the tall angel monument that had stood in the Town Square for more than a hundred years. He set the bags he'd been carrying down, then took her hand and said, "Hope you're hungry."

She turned to see Reverend Strong watching them as he passed by, his curiosity clearly evident on his face. She blushed. Josie pulled her hand away. Cole didn't miss a beat.

"Afternoon, Preacher," he said. "Fine day for a picnic, wouldn't you say?"

*"Harumph."* The pastor of the First Baptist Church of Angel Ridge had to clear his throat before he spoke. Josie noticed that he wore his usual dark suit and clerical collar. "Indeed it is." He nodded to her and said, "Dr. Allen, Cole. Good day," before continuing down the brick sidewalk.

Josie's blush deepened. "Pastor Strong."

"Let's eat." Cole dropped to one knee and tried to pull her down beside him, but Josie resisted. "Something wrong?" He squinted into the sunshine as he looked up at her.

She looked around at all the people milling about, then lowered herself beside him. "Maybe we should have picked a less busy place for a picnic," she whispered.

"Well, I can't say the thought didn't cross my mind. But I figured you might think it improper if I took you somewhere . . ." he paused, and then added, "more secluded."

The timbre of his voice dipped to a soft bass on that last word. He was probably right. Any more time alone with the compelling Cole Craig, and it'd be hard telling what she'd do. She should be working. She'd decided last night she couldn't afford any distractions right now. The handsome, sexy-as-sin man sitting so close beside her was beyond a distraction. And yet, here she was.

"Cole, we are adults." Josie laughed to cover her mixed emotions.

He leaned in so that his face was only inches from hers. "So, you do want to be alone with me?" He took her hand and brought it to his lips for a lingering caress along her knuckles.

"Oh . . ." she breathed just before her heart tripped into double time.

"How's that chicken salad?" Dixie Ferguson asked.

Startled, Josie sat back on her heels.

"I'm sure it's as good as it always is, Dix," Cole said, shooting her a look that could wound.

Dixie nodded. Josie thought she saw her wink, but decided she must have imagined it. Dixie didn't slow her hurried pace as she crossed the Town Square carrying a large box. "Glad to hear it," she called out, then continued down Main Street toward Ferguson's.

The bag with a Ferguson's Diner logo on the front rustled as Cole reached in to get the food. "There's pickle wedges and fruit salad, too." He handed Josie a thick sandwich wrapped in wax paper. "What's the matter, Josie Lee? You look a little flustered."

Her hand fluttered in the vicinity of the collar of her white, cotton dress shirt. Jeez, it was warm.

"Why don't you take off that suit coat and relax," he suggested before offering her a paper cup filled with iced tea.

Relax? She looked around. That would be difficult — no impossible — with half the population of Angel Ridge bearing down on them.

"You're not embarrassed to be seen with me, are you?"

Josie turned to Cole then. He had a look of vulnerability on his face that surprised her, and pulled at her heart. "Cole, no," she said immediately, squeezing his hand as she spoke. Then amended, "Well, it is a little embarrassing, but not for the reasons you're thinking."

"What reasons, then?" he asked.

He still had that look on his face. Josie removed her jacket with his help, set it aside, and then tried to make herself more comfortable. "Cole," she began, "this is our first," she paused searching for the right word, "public outing together. I mean, I know we went to the diner last night, but we were all alone except for Dixie. Here, I just feel like everyone's staring. Like they're curious about what we're doing. It's a small town."

A rakish smile pulled at the corner of Cole's mouth, making him look devilishly handsome despite his fair, angelic features. "Are you worried about your reputation?"

She toyed with the cuff of her sleeve and laughed. "Should I be?"

He leaned forward and touched her knee. The intense look in his eyes, combined with his touch, nearly undid her.

"If you give me the opportunity, we could sure find out," he said softly.

"Cole! I got that new level in that you ordered." Mr. DeFoe from the hardware stood by their picnic blanket, smiling down at them as if he hadn't just interrupted a sensually charged moment.

Cole's frustration was telling in the way a muscle ticked in his jaw. Josie had to admit, she felt a little relieved by the interruption. She undid a button on her blouse and fanned herself with the fabric.

"Thanks, Mr. DeFoe," Cole said, but didn't stop looking at her as he spoke. "I'll come by later and pick it up."

"Fine lookin' level. I've had it out playing with it all mornin'. Yep, it's as true as true can be."

Cole just smiled as he ran his fingertips around her kneecap. "Glad to hear it. See you later today, then."

"Oh!" The short and stocky man took a step back, as if he just realized he *had* interrupted something. "Yes, well, maybe you can have a look at those shelves in the back of my store when you come by. They could use some shoring up."

Cole sighed. "Be glad to."

"Well, then. *Ahem.* Yes — Miss Josie." The older man nodded at Josie.

She brushed Cole's hand away from her knee. "Mr. DeFoe."

When the man finally moved on, Josie and Cole laughed. Glad that the atmosphere was slightly less charged, she unwrapped her sandwich and took a bite. "*Mmm . . .* there is nothing better than Dixie's chicken salad." She sipped her tea. "Except for maybe her iced tea." The ultra sweet amber liquid tasted like nectar.

He bit into his sandwich as well. "Dixie's the best cook around, that's for sure."

After they had both eaten most of their sandwiches, Cole said, "You know, Miss Estelee agreed that the angel monument was just the spot for us to have a picnic," Cole said.

Surprised, Josie asked, "You and Miss Estelee discussed our having lunch together?"

"Well, you see, she called me this mornin' and insisted I come by and trim her boxwoods. Let's just say she was in a talkative mood today. She actually suggested that I bring you here."

"Really?"

"Yeah. Said that she used to sit on that park bench over there with her only love."

"I didn't know she ever married," Josie said, a little breathless.

"Don't believe she did, but she says if a fella wants to start things off right with a lady, he should take her to the angel monument early on." He paused, then said, "You know, it was erected just before the Civil

War to watch over and protect the town. Miss Estelee's family commissioned a sculptor for the angel. My great-great grandfather made the brick pedestal he stands on."

"I had no idea." He had her head swimming from his talk of only loves and beginnings. Why did things suddenly feel like they were spinning out of control?

"Miss Estelee also puts in the flowers here every spring."

"She plants them herself?" Josie asked, surprised.

"Nah. I set 'em out for her. She always chooses something red."

She smiled. "It must be her favorite color. I remember her wearing a new red dress to Christmas Eve services every year."

Josie glanced up at the angel monument. The warrior angel stood passive, holding a sword by its hilt, point down, a vigilant look on his handsome face. She suddenly realized that Cole bore a striking resemblance to the winged man the artist had immortalized in bronze.

"Do you look like your great-great grandfather, Cole?"

He shrugged. "I don't know. Why?"

She pointed up at the statue. "You look like the angel. I was just wondering if the sculptor maybe used your great-great grandfather as a model."

He laughed and stared up at the angel. "Who knows?"

"Tell me something, Cole. Do you believe there are angels in Angel Ridge?"

He grinned, "What? You wondering if they've appeared to every generation of Craigs since the town was founded?"

"Well, yes," she admitted.

Cole took her hand and softly said, "I'm looking at the only angel I've ever seen in Angel Ridge."

The foot traffic seemed to die down. The tension between her and Cole was so thick, Josie found it difficult to breathe.

"Maybe we should meet at one o'clock tomorrow," he suggested, his voice husky.

All of a sudden, she couldn't focus on anything but Cole's lips so close to hers. Josie nodded. "Maybe there'd be less people around later in the day."

He grinned mischievously. "I thought I'd just take you to that clearing up in the tall pines. It's nice and quiet up there."

"I don't think I've ever seen it," she admitted. Of course, she'd heard of it. It was kind of like Angel Ridge's version of Lovers' Lane. All couples went there to make out at least once in the course of their courtship.

He touched her face. "I'd love to be the

one to show it to you."

Without thinking, she leaned into his touch. She couldn't deny that she'd like to find out what it would be like to be kissed. Really kissed. She was sure it would be nothing like the kisses she'd shared with the men she'd dated in the past. Those kisses had been nothing special. And she had to admit that being kissed by someone like Cole made the prospect much more exciting. She'd worry about the consequences later.

He slowly leaned forward. *This is it. It's going to happen. He's going to kiss me.* But instead of her mouth, his lips brushed warmly across her cheek.

She sighed, disappointed. Covering his hand with hers, she pressed it against her cheek. She'd like nothing better than to kiss him, but she was old-fashioned enough to want him to make the first move. Still, they needed more privacy than the Town Square provided.

So, she suggested, "Maybe you could show me that clearing up in the tall pines . . . now."

# CHAPTER 4

Josie stared up at Cole. Desire had darkened her golden eyes to a beguiling shade of hot amber. He shifted. Taking Josie up to the lovers' clearing would be a dream come true. But Josie wasn't the kind of woman who did things on impulse. Not without regretting it later. Still, he didn't want her to feel rejected.

"What about work?" he asked. Maybe if he steered her attention back to business. . . .

"I could call Teresa and tell her I'm taking the rest of the afternoon off," she offered.

She wasn't helping at all. She turned her head and pressed her warm, soft lips against his palm. He wanted to kiss her so badly he couldn't see straight. He grabbed a fist full of the blanket. The wool scratched his palm. Dear Lord. He needed a cold shower. Now.

Josie looked up at him with a dreamy expression in her eyes that he claimed all for his own. Energy seemed to crackle all around them. He inched forward, slowly. Their noses touched and they angled their heads in anticipation of the kiss. But just as his lips would have touched hers, a loud noise exploded inside his head. The earth vibrated beneath them.

God must have heard his earlier prayer, because the heavens opened and a cold, drenching rain shocked them apart.

"Oh!" Josie exclaimed, jerking her head back. "It's raining!"

Cole looked up at the darkened sky, laughing as icy needles of rain stung his face. "Imagine that. We didn't even notice those thunderheads rolling in."

"No wonder the streets were deserted all of the sudden."

"Let's get out of this downpour." He had to shout to be heard above the pounding rain. It seemed to come down harder by the second.

They stood, and he folded everything up in the blanket. Then they ran for cover under the blue awning outside the bank. Everyone inside stared at them curiously. Cole noticed that Josie's white blouse had become quite transparent. He stared as well — for a second. Then he got hold of himself. *I have to get her out of here.*

"My truck's parked right over there. Why don't I take you home so you can get changed?"

Josie opened her mouth to respond, but fell silent as an old blue Buick pulled up alongside the sidewalk near where they stood.

The town's retired high school history teacher, Mrs. Church, rolled down the window. She had to nearly shout to be heard above the pouring rain. "Hello, Josie. I saw you standing over here and thought you might like a ride back to the library. You know, the Historical Society meeting begins in five minutes." The little gray-haired lady pursed her lips, and after looking Josie over from head to toe observed, "Josephine, you are all wet."

"Yes," Josie finally found her voice. Looking down at herself, her eyes widened and she crossed her arms over her chest.

The old woman's eyes narrowed. "Who is that there with you? Is that the Craig boy?"

Before he could speak, Josie said, "Yes, ma'am. Cole was just about to help me get out of these wet clothes."

*"Humph!"*

Cole couldn't keep from chuckling.

Josie stammered. "I — I mean change. Take me home so I can *change* out of these wet clothes."

"I would think that you should," Mrs. Church said.

"I'll join you and the other ladies in just a few minutes, Mrs. Church."

"I shall inform Mrs. McKay that you will be tardy," Mrs. Church said in the stern, clipped voice of a schoolteacher. "I'm very disappointed in you, Josephine." She rolled up her window and continued down the street at a restrained five miles per hour, her head barely visible above the steering wheel.

Josie dropped her head into her hands and said, "Can this get any more humiliating?"

"Come on. I'll drive you home." Cole grasped her elbow, and they sprinted through the rain to his truck.

After they'd settled themselves inside, he tossed the wet picnic blanket containing the remains of their lunch behind the seat. Everything had been going so well, but now, it seemed things couldn't get any worse.

He grabbed his denim jacket and settled it around Josie's shoulders. She looked thoroughly embarrassed and withdrawn. He'd be lucky if she would agree to ever see him again.

She'd been right. Taking her to such a public spot had been a bad idea. He'd only wanted to test the waters to see if she'd mind being seen with him in public. He should have noticed the storm clouds rolling in, but when he got around Josie, he blocked out everything but her. Being dog tired from a late night didn't help either.

He started the truck. They completed the short drive to her house in silence. The rain hadn't let up at all when he pulled into her drive and shut off the engine. He rested his arm along the back of the bench seat and studied her.

Her hair frizzed around her face. One fat curl had pulled away from that knot she'd twisted her hair into at the back of her head and now hung enticingly against her cheek, down along her neck, finally resting on the front of his jacket. He remembered the way she'd looked at him earlier, her eyes begging him to kiss her. Watching her now in the seclusion of his truck cab with the windows steaming up, the desire to kiss her intensified.

He reached out and touched her cheek. "Josie . . ." His voice sounded hoarse, even to his own ears.

She glanced up at him, then turned away, but not before he saw the closed look in her eyes.

"Don't." Cole squeezed her shoulder. He couldn't bear the thought of her shutting herself off from him for any reason. Not now.

She closed her eyes. "I forgot the Historical Society was meeting this afternoon. I have to change and get back to work."

He grasped her hand before she could leave. "Will I see you tomorrow?"

"I don't know, Cole. I'm really behind at work."

He wasn't about to give up on her. Not because of a little embarrassment. There was definitely something between them. Today had proven it. "How 'bout I call you later?"

She sighed, but didn't answer. Cole reached out and turned her face toward him with a finger at her chin. When her eyes met his, he said, "I wish I knew what to say to take us back to fifteen minutes ago."

She chewed on her lower lip, but hadn't gotten out of the truck yet. That encouraged him to continue.

He teased a stray curl at her temple. "You look real pretty wet, Josie Lee."

She tried to tuck the hair that had fallen out of that knot behind her ears. "I'm sure I'm a mess."

"A beautiful mess."

Cole smoothed his hand from her cheek to the back of her neck. He very much wanted to take the pins out of her hair and watch it fall across her shoulders and down her back. He shifted closer to her. Josie shivered.

"You're freezing," he whispered. He slipped his hands inside the jacket he'd settled loosely around her shoulders earlier and rubbed her arms through her wet shirt.

"Cole . . ."

*"Mmm?"* She smelled like some kind of wildflower growing in the meadow on his farm. He inhaled deeply, then pressed his lips against the pounding pulse at the side of her neck. So, the town librarian wasn't completely unaffected by his touch.

"I should go . . ." she said as she edged closer to the door, effectively breaking the contact.

Cole settled his hands on her waist, stalling her retreat. "Would you like me to wait while you change? I could drive you back to work."

"No. I have my car in the garage."

He pulled her a little closer until their thighs aligned. "You're sure?"

Her gaze skidded from his face to the wet shirt stretched across his chest and back again just before she pushed away from him, sucked in a ragged breath, and said, "I'm sure I have to go. Now."

She may have mixed feelings on the matter, but duty called. Her work came first. Had to come first. He wanted her back in his arms, but the timing was all wrong. Factor in that she was still reluctant to let him get too close. She'd have to come to him in her own time. This much was becoming clear.

"Okay. I'll call you later?" He held his breath while he waited for her response.

"Cole?"

"Yeah?"

"Can I be honest with you?"

"Sure," he said cautiously.

"I know that I've probably given you the impression that I — well, that I may want us to be more than friends."

"That don't bother me a bit." His heart pounded at the thought of them being much more than friends.

She looked away from him. "It bothers me."

His racing heart ground to a halt. This conversation was going from bad to worse. "Why?"

"Because I can't afford the distraction right now."

Oh, yeah. She was clearly conflicted on the issue. The way she chewed on her thumbnail was telling. The way she reacted to him was also telling. Cole felt his smile return. "So, I'm a distraction?"

Josie rolled her eyes. "Yes," she admitted. "I should be paying attention to what's on my calendar and working out the kinks in my computer program instead of letting you ply me with Dixie's cooking."

He squeezed the back of her neck. "Stop worrying about that program."

She pushed the damp hair back off her forehead. "How can I? The system has to be operational in less than two weeks. The way things are looking now, I'll be unemployed by then."

"It'll be working like a charm by tomorrow."

"I wish I had your confidence." She looked at her watch. "I really have to go."

When Cole reached over to open the door for her, his chest pressed up against hers. She inhaled sharply. He enjoyed the contact, too. After he leaned back, she slowly slid across the seat, but turned back before getting out. "Oh, my jacket. I almost forgot."

They both looked at the soaked blanket lying in a wad behind the seat. He imagined it smeared with chicken salad and sticky fruit. "Why don't you keep mine. I'll drop yours off at the cleaners."

She smiled then, some of her good humor

returning. "Thank you for lunch."

He smiled, too. "You're welcome."

On impulse, he leaned over and gave her a quick kiss on the cheek. It wasn't anywhere near the kind of kiss he wanted to give her. The kind he'd dreamed of giving her while he'd lain awake most of the night, but it seemed the safest thing to do at the moment. He comforted himself in knowing there'd be other opportunities. He'd see to that.

She smiled a smile that women had used to ensnare men since the beginning of time. Cole had to admit as he watched her run up the brick sidewalk to her front door, she had him good and trapped.

As soon as the meeting of the Historical Society ended, Josie escaped to her office and closed the door. The looks she'd gotten from Mrs. Church and Mrs. McKay during the long meeting could have wounded.

She had just sat down at her desk when the door to her office opened and Mrs. McKay swept into the room. "Here you are."

*Like mother, like son.* "Mrs. McKay."

"I need to speak with you, Josephine." If the woman pursed her lips any tighter, they'd shatter.

Though it grated, she would play at being contrite. It was expected. "I'm sorry I was late to the meeting, Mrs. McKay. It won't happen again." No need making excuses.

"See that it doesn't. Now about the matter I wished to discuss with you . . ." The painfully thin, elderly matron lowered herself to perch on the edge of the leather wing chair positioned in front of Josie's desk.

"Yes?"

"Josephine, I know you have been away from Angel Ridge for some time. You've lived in larger cities these last years where a young lady's conduct is not so closely scrutinized."

She paused. Josie couldn't imagine where this was going, but she had a sinking feeling it would end somewhere in the vicinity of Cole Craig.

"Here in Angel Ridge, there is a certain code of conduct that a lady of your station is expected to follow."

"A lady of my station?"

"Certainly. A young lady of breeding and education who is an esteemed member of the community should conduct herself accordingly. She should consort with gentlemen of similar status and experience, attend the proper social functions, become involved in philanthropic pursuits by joining the right clubs, serving on the right committees."

Josie must have appeared completely baffled, because Mrs. McKay continued, "The Garden Club, the Association of University Women, the Junior League, to name a few."

"I see."

"Good. Then I need not state that associating with young men from the wrong side of the ridge would be frowned upon by the members of The McKay Foundation board. The Foundation that funded your education and provides the salary for your position here."

Josie seethed, but said, "I understand." She got it loud and clear. They owned her, just like this town had owned her all her life.

"Good. I'm glad we had this little chat. Now, how is the new cataloging program working? Are we on schedule for the Memorial Day debut?"

"Everything is going as planned," she lied. It would be a cold day before she admitted that anything was amiss to this insufferable woman.

"Splendid. I'll let you return to your work, then. I expect you'll stay late to compensate for the time you lost today. Good day."

Josie's first impulse after the door clicked shut behind the witch was to hurl a crystal paperweight at it. She held back only because it was the one her parents had given her when she'd won her first regional spelling bee.

How dare she? How dare that woman lecture her on appropriate conduct? Social status indeed. She made it sound as if this was England or something, and she a titled lady. Obviously Mrs. McKay was still living in another decade. Another century even.

Josie stabbed at the power button on her computer and waited an eternity for it to boot.

"Dr. Allen?" Teresa had opened Josie's door only far enough to look inside.

"Come in, Teresa. And call me Josie."

"Oh. I couldn't possibly. Mrs. McKay —"

"Look, Teresa, Mrs. McKay may sign the checks, but I'll not be her protégé, regardless of what she dictates."

"O — kay . . ." Teresa said slowly.

"I'm sorry, Teresa. I've had nothing but a string of bad days and my mood is not the best. What did you need?"

"*Um,* I hate to tell you this, but the network's crashed again."

Josie rubbed her forehead. "Not again.

This is the last thing I need."

"I'm sorry. I've tried all the usual things, but nothing's working."

"You've checked all the cables?"

"Yes."

Josie sighed. "Have everyone log off the network, and I'll see what I can do."

Teresa wrung her hands. "How will we check out books?"

"We'll have to go back to doing it the old-fashioned way. Have the clerks log every book with their locater numbers so that they can input them when I get the system back up."

"Yes, ma'am."

"Teresa?"

"I'm sorry. Sure thing, Jo— Josie."

"Thanks, Teresa."

"You're burnin' the midnight oil, Dixie." Cole settled himself on a stool at the counter of Ferguson's and helped himself to a doughnut from the covered cake plate sitting too close to resist.

"Those pies and cakes you people consume don't bake themselves magically." She gave him a sweeping look. "Well, you look slightly better than you did earlier. I take it the picnic went well."

Cole bit into his doughnut. "Depends on

your definition of *well*."

"Okay. You had fabulous food, a picture perfect day, and the woman of your dreams sitting with you on a picnic blanket. Surely even you couldn't screw that up."

"It rained, ending the picnic abruptly." He wiped his mouth with a napkin and added, "How 'bout a cup of coffee?"

"Did it rain?"

The false innocent look on Dixie's face said it all. He pointed a finger at her. "You knew!" He slapped the counter. The television in the diner was always set to the Weather Channel or CNN.

She leaned in. "Gettin' all wet and havin' to take the woman to her house to change can't have been all that bad."

"Well now, that did happen, but there was a snag. A couple of them."

"Such as."

"Such as, first, we had to run for cover under the awning of the bank. I'm sure someone scurried straight to Mrs. McKay about it. Then there was Old Maid Church, who just happened by on her way to the Historical Society Meeting at the library and saw us. A meeting Josie was supposed to attend. Needless to say, she was late."

"I'll just bet Mrs. McKay gave poor Josie *you know what* over it, too."

"I'd say that's a safe assumption. I'd also say it's likely she never wants to see me again."

Dixie looked at her watch. "Closin' time. I bet Josie's still holed up over at the library like she is most nights."

"Yep."

"Did you call her earlier?"

"No."

She propped a hand on her narrow hip. "Well, why not?"

"I been busy." He wiped his hands on his napkin. "I had to go home and change after that farce of a picnic —"

"It can't have been all bad."

Well, there had been moments . . . He frowned and continued. "Then Mr. DeFoe had a mess of shelves I spent all afternoon rightin'. Then I had to go back home —"

Dixie snapped him with a rolled up dishtowel. "I didn't miss that cow-eyed look on your face when you got sidetracked a minute ago. Get your be-hind over to the library right now, Cole Craig."

"She ain't gonna want to see me again today."

"Really, men can be so dense. Let me spell it out for you. You'd better get on over there and do some damage control, or you may never see her again. Give her too much time to think, and I guarantee, she'll be thinkin' things that won't be good for your buddin' relationship."

"What do you care, Dix?"

She wiped the counter with her towel. "Well, you know, it's springtime, young love and all."

Cole didn't miss the sadness that clouded her eyes. "How's Susan?" Dixie's best friend since childhood and the mayor's wife had just been diagnosed with breast cancer. The whole town had been upset by the grave prognosis.

"As well as can be expected. She's tough. She'll fight this, just like you oughta be fightin' for what you want." It was her turn to point at him now. "Life's too short."

She was right. As usual.

"You got any coconut cream pie back there?"

"Does your dog have fleas? What do you need pie for?"

"If all else fails, I thought I'd ply her with sweets."

"Good thinkin'."

Dixie dished the pie into a styrofoam container and handed it to him. "There. Now get goin'."

"Yes, ma'am."

As Cole walked the short distance to the

library, he hoped Josie wouldn't shut and lock the window in his face. Maybe if he helped her with her program, she'd be grateful enough to go out with him on a real date. He smiled and quickened his pace.

Josie sat back and kneaded the aching muscles in her neck. It had taken hours to get the network operational again this afternoon. She'd been testing the catalog portion of the program, but every time she thought they might be ready to test it with the Internet portion of the program, the system crashed. The problem was that these computers just couldn't handle the amount of information they'd been inputting. She didn't even want to think about what would happen when they tried to process the graphics in the website. If she could only get the two portions to connect. For the last couple of hours, she'd been back to doing what she should have been doing all day — trying to figure out was wrong with the programming.

This time the tapping on the window didn't even surprise her. She turned to see Cole standing outside with a big grin on his face. She rolled over and unlocked the window. After she opened it, he swung himself up onto the sill.

"Hey, Josie Lee. Working late again, I see." He leaned back against the window casing and gave her a look that had probably just melted her hard drive.

With her elbow on her desk, she propped her head in her hand and stared at him. Mrs. McKay would have a fit if she could see this. The knowledge gave Josie perverse pleasure. Didn't every good girl have a secret longing to be bad? Looking at Cole, all the naughty possibilities that could fill a girl's fantasies seemed limitless.

Refocusing, she said, "Yes, I'm always working. What do you have there?"

He held a white container aloft. "Coconut cream pie."

"How is it you know all my favorites?"

He shrugged and kept smiling. "Just lucky, I guess." He handed her the container. "Still havin' trouble with your program?"

"Yes," she nodded. "I was just about to throw in the towel for tonight."

"*Aw*, don't do that."

"I've never been so frustrated with anything in all my life." She set the pie aside and rubbed the back of her neck. "I'm so tired."

"Sounds like you need a helping hand. First things first."

Cole shifted and stood, then approached

her in measured steps. He moved with the natural rolling gate of an athlete, filling the room with his presence. Disquieted by his nearness, Josie dragged in a deep breath. Her nostrils filled with the enticing scent of his cologne, and her heart jumped and hammered against her rib cage. He was a full-blown, living, breathing fantasy.

"Oh my," she whispered, then swallowed hard.

He'd changed into clean blue jeans and a red polo style shirt. His blond hair, damp from the shower, was tied back with a thin piece of leather. He'd shaved, too. She had to admit, as good as he looked, she'd liked the more elemental Cole she'd had in her office earlier. Hair down, stubble shadowing his jaw, the smell of the outdoors and his own natural musky scent clinging to his skin.

He pivoted her chair to face the computer screen, then rested his warm hands on her shoulders. When he began massaging the kinks, Josie flinched. The muscles were so tight, just touching them was painful.

"I'm sorry," he apologized. "Just give it a minute."

After that moment passed, she moaned her pleasure. He possessed magical fingers.

"How's that feel?" he said softly, his lips

brushing her ear.

"Heavenly."

With one hand on the arm of her chair and the other running lightly from her shoulder to her wrist, Cole kept his head on the same level as hers. She was more aware of him than any man she'd ever known. His face was so close to hers, she'd only have to turn her head slightly to run her lips up the column of his throat.

"You know, I'm pretty good at fixing things, and I did promise you yesterday we'd tackle this. So, why don't you tell me about the problems you're having?"

He stared at her computer screen. *It must seem like Greek to him,* she thought. Sure, he was good at fixing things, but this was a state of the art computer program. Not something for a handyman to fix. Besides, the last thing she wanted to think about with him this close was work.

She turned her head and spoke softly near his ear. "It's complicated, Cole. Technical."

*"Hmm,"* he murmured, then swung his magnificent blue-eyed gaze in her direction. "Too complicated for someone like me, you mean."

"Cole, no. I —" Josie immediately began to apologize for insulting him, but he just smiled and turned back to the computer.

"The purpose of the program is to catalog just the books?" he asked.

Josie frowned, trying to concentrate on the words when all she wanted to do was feel. "No. It's all inclusive," she managed. "Periodicals, research titles, genealogical material and the town archives, newspapers —"

"With Internet access?" Though he continued massaging her shoulders, his gaze was fixed on the screen.

"*Hmm?* Oh, yes. Internet. Everything in the catalog will be accessible through a website, so it has to interface."

"That's the problem, then."

"Excuse me?"

"The loop to include Internet access isn't complete." Cole pointed at the screen into the maze of programming language and pinpointed the area Josie had isolated as the source of the problem.

Josie tore her attention away from the man next to her and slid her glasses onto her nose. She leaned forward.

"The way it's written now would cause the program to freeze when it hits this string of commands."

"Exactly, and since I wasn't hooked up to the Internet during the trials I did with the program, it didn't matter before now," Josie breathed.

"May I?" he asked.

"Certainly." When Cole reached around her from behind to type something into the keyboard, encircling her with his strong arms, Josie's skin tingled where his arms brushed against hers. She watched in fascinated wonder as he added a simple string of commands to the area he'd indicated, then pressed "Enter." Another string of commands appeared on the screen, and the program scrolled to the end.

He typed in a few more commands to close the loop then said, "Why don't you try running it now?"

Amazed and speechless, she ran the program. It worked like a dream. She took off her glasses and looked up at him. "How did you do that?"

He shrugged and slid his hands into his back pockets. "It was simple, really. Sometimes you just need somebody who can see things fresh."

"But I don't understand."

"You mean you don't understand how a guy like me could know anything about computers?"

That's exactly what Josie was thinking, and she hated herself for it. She was making surface assumptions about Cole based on the town's perception of him. Again. She didn't want to turn into a bitter, old prejudiced woman like Mrs. McKay. Of all people, she should know better than to pigeonhole a human being when she'd been caged all her life.

"Where did you learn how to do this?"

He shrugged. "I took a couple of courses at the community center in Maryville. Then, I learned a few things on my own by playing around and reading a few books."

Josie smiled and turned back to the computer. "Let me just run a few tests."

While she ran her tests, Cole stood back and watched. The program performed in every way that it was designed to perform. Now if she only had the computer power she needed to really make this thing cook . . . After a few moments, she stood and faced him. "It's perfect. I don't know how to thank you."

"*Aw,* it was nothin'." He looked away, embarrassed.

Josie touched his arm. When their eyes met, she said, "Cole Craig, you are truly an amazing man. In two days, you've managed to help me avert disaster at home and at work."

He took her hand in his, and she felt the familiar heat course through her.

"Plus I saved you from starvation. Don't forget that."

"How could I? Thank you."

"It was my pleasure."

With the old-world charm of a gentleman, he brought her hand to his lips, and without breaking eye contact, kissed it. Josie willed her knees to work, but gave herself a little help by grasping the edge of her desk. Again, she wondered what would happen if he pressed those magical lips to hers. . . .

"How 'bout I walk you home?" he asked, his voice soft and low.

"I'd like that," she said without hesitation. Mrs. McKay could take a flying leap. She was fascinated by this man who'd never finished high school, but could repair a flaw in a complicated computer program as easily as he repaired a pipe under her house. She wanted to know the real Cole Craig, because he clearly was not who he appeared to be. She wondered what she would find if the layers were peeled away and the real Cole revealed.

# CHAPTER 5

"Another beautiful Angel Ridge night," Josie said. She lifted her face to the sky.

"Beautiful," Cole agreed. He'd never seen anything as lovely. Looking at her, he understood what inspired Lord Byron to write, *She walks in beauty, like the night of cloudless climes and starry skies; and all that's best of dark and bright meet in her aspect and her eyes.*

Above all, Cole wanted a chance with her. He knew that wouldn't happen as long as she was preoccupied with that program. So, he'd fixed it. He'd taken a risk revealing his knowledge to her the way he had. And he'd lied to her about how he learned to use computers. He hated lying to her, but he really had no choice.

He knew what people on the ridge thought of him. That he was only good for repairing what needed fixing with people's homes and businesses and such. Never once had anyone stopped to consider that he might have a mind. Hopes. Dreams.

He could honestly say that none of that had ever really mattered to him. He'd come to terms with people's prejudices early in life and had tried not to let that define who he was as a person. But he was finding that what Josie Allen thought of him meant everything. When he looked into her eyes, he saw an openness. Her mind, though colored by the town's preconceived notions of those who lived below the ridge, seemed open to finding out who he really was.

Beside him she smiled and whirled in a circle. He couldn't help laughing.

"I'm so happy the program is working that I could just sing!"

"What's stoppin' you?" They turned off Main Street onto Ridge Road. Tall, old Victorian homes played peek-a-boo with large trees standing in front yards. "Everyone's tucked safely inside their houses. Nobody but me and the crickets are listening."

*Lord, she was a thing of beauty.*

She chanced a look at him and confessed, "I can't carry a tune."

"Me neither," he confided, "but that don't usually stop me." And with that, he launched into a rollicking off-key rendition of *Chantilly Lace* that had Josie giggling until they walked up the steps to her wide front porch.

Without giving it a thought, Cole wrapped an arm around her waist and swung her in a wide circle. When he stopped spinning her and set her feet back on the ground, she smiled the sweetest smile up at him. He didn't know if he was lightheaded from the spinning or that look on Josie Allen's face.

A golden-red curl had fallen out of its coil and lay against her cheek. He brushed it back in a perfect moment that seemed suspended in time. Then, he leaned down and did what he'd dreamed of doing since she'd returned to Angel Ridge.

He kissed her.

But this was no young boy's fantasy of a girl that seemed just out of his reach. This was as real as it got.

After a moment's contact with Josie's lips warm and soft beneath his, Cole wrapped his arms around her waist and pulled her close up against his chest. His heart filled near to bursting with longing for her, but he cautioned himself to take it slow lest the dream in his arms vanish. Still, he nearly lost all control when she pulled the leather tie out of his hair and sank her fingers into it. Before he could recover, she gently sucked on his bottom lip.

A slow burn started in his gut and spread lower as he touched his tongue to hers. She sighed and melted against him. He buried his hand into the knot of hair at the back of her head. Hairpins bounced across the porch as it tumbled down his arm in a silken curtain. He pulled his lips from hers then and pressed his mouth to the pounding pulse at the side of her throat. A smell like roses in the heat of July filled his senses until he was intoxicated with everything about her.

"Josie," he groaned as he swept his hands down the curve of her back.

Somewhere in the muddle of his mind, he realized that she was pushing against his chest. Pushing him away. Cole relaxed his hold on her, then stepped back.

Letting go of her was one of the hardest things he'd ever had to do. He just stood there and looked at her. What a glorious sight she was with her hair hanging loose down her back and across her shoulders; her lips red and wet from his kiss.

She touched a hand to her mouth . . . tried to smooth the tangle of her hair. "I think you should go."

"Josie . . ." He reached out to touch her, but she moved back. Out of his reach. Oh man, had he read the signals wrong? Had he stepped over the line with her?

"Please. I . . ."

She began to pace. She seemed totally confused. Definitely agitated. He wasn't about to leave things like this. "Josie," he coaxed, "let's sit down over here and talk."

"No. No, I don't think that's a good idea."

"Why?"

"Because I'm not sure what's happening between us, and I'm not sure it should. Happen," she added for clarification.

"What makes you say that?"

She'd drifted toward the back corner of the porch.

He followed. "We've been having a good time together, haven't we?"

"Well — I suppose," she agreed, if a bit cautiously.

"So we had a little kiss." He shrugged. "It seemed natural. What's the harm in it?" What they'd just shared had by no stretch of the imagination been just a simple kiss. But, he thought it best to downplay things for the time being. At least until she'd had time to sort it all out.

But then she tossed back at him exactly what he'd been thinking. She turned and hit him square in the face with, "That was no simple kiss, Cole Craig. That was — was —"

"Incredible?" he supplied.

She raked an unsteady hand through her hair. "I didn't expect this. Didn't mean for it to happen."

Okay, it seemed like she'd shifted to the big picture now. He chose to ignore that, keeping to his game plan. "But it did. And there's no need in gettin' all upset over it," he said softly. Downplay. Keep it light.

She still faced him, all five feet nothing of her, determined fire lighting her eyes. "How can you say that? You and I have no business kissing each other that way."

"Why not?" Cole ground his teeth together. Had he read her wrong? Was she about to tell him something that interpreted meant he wasn't good enough for her?

He was already forming a counter-argument when she surprised him by saying, "We hardly know each other."

Cole smiled and breathed a bit easier. "We've known each other since we were kids, Josie."

"Before yesterday, I hadn't really spoken to you since we were kids. Which proves my point. We don't really *know* each other."

He smiled and wiggled his eyebrows. "What better way to get to know a person?"

"Cole!"

Time to get serious . . . for a moment anyway. "I enjoyed kissing you." He paused to let that sink in, and then added, "If you'd let yourself, you'd have to admit you enjoyed kissing me, too."

"You're changing the subject."

She began pacing again. He definitely had the town librarian out of sorts. He smiled. It was a start.

Cole crossed his arms then rubbed his bottom lip with his thumb. It still tingled from her kiss. After a moment, he softly asked, "Does it bother you that I come from the back side of the ridge, Josie?"

She stopped pacing and looked up at him. "No." Her response had been immediate. Emphatic. "No, it doesn't bother *me.*"

They were moving in the right direction, but Cole knew they weren't out of the woods yet. "You worried about what people will say?"

"No. Well, maybe a little . . . Oh, I don't know."

She pushed her hair back from her face and turned away from him. He walked up to stand close behind her. "Is that all it is?"

"No."

He touched her shoulder. "Tell me."

She turned back to him, then looked away

again. "This is just a little sudden, Cole. I guess you could say my behavior with you has been, well, out of character. This just isn't like me. I mean, I don't do anything without thinking it through. And I certainly don't go around casually kissing men I hardly know, or haven't seen in years. Okay, I don't go around casually kissing men period."

He stepped forward, pleased to see that she didn't retreat. "It wasn't something I planned, Josie. It just happened. That's not to say that I'm sorry it happened. Still, there's no need in reading more into it than there is."

Josie nodded her agreement, but worried her lower lip with her teeth.

After a moment of silence, he added, "I wouldn't mind gettin' to know you better, if you'd be agreeable."

"What if we find out we have nothing in common? I mean, we come from such different backgrounds."

"No worries." He wrapped a long red curl around his finger pulling her incrementally closer as he did. "I've always had a soft spot for pretty girls with curly red hair."

A slow smile turned her serious expression into a look that started his pulse back racing.

"Tomorrow's Saturday," Cole said. "How 'bout I pick you up around three and we drive out to Vonore?"

Josie laughed and shook her head. The movement made her hair slide off his finger. He put his hand in his pocket.

"What?" he asked.

"I was just wondering what could be going on in Vonore on a Saturday night to warrant investigation."

"Well now, that shows how much you know, *Dr.* Allen. It just so happens that the Chicago boys are in town."

"Sounds like a gang of bank robbers."

"Boy, for a smart lady, you sure don't know much," he teased. "So, I'll pick you up about three?"

She hesitated a moment, as if weighing the wisdom of pursuing their association. But in the end she said, "You're not going to tell me anything else? Just that we're going to Vonore?"

He'd take that as a *yes.* "Oh, yeah. Wear something casual. You got any jeans?"

"Well, I might have to dig, but I'm sure they're somewhere. Maybe buried in the back of a drawer."

"Well, find 'em and wear 'em," he said with a big grin.

She hesitated again. Cole held his breath.

"Okay. Three o'clock."

He breathed again. "I'll pick you up here, then?"

"Sure."

Cole leaned down and gave Josie a long, soft kiss. When he finally lifted his head, he said, "See you tomorrow," then turned to go.

"Cole?"

He stopped on the bottom step and looked back up at her.

"Thank you . . . for everything."

He grinned and said, "Anytime."

Then he walked down the sidewalk back to town whistling *Chantilly Lace*.

The next afternoon, Cole strolled up the walk to Josie's house carrying a mixed bouquet of roses he'd cut from his mother's garden. He wore his best pair of jeans and a new long-sleeved white button-up shirt. He hoped to get his denim jacket back from Josie for later when it got cool.

He jumped up onto the porch, skipping several steps in the process, and turned the crank on the old-timey doorbell. It made a buzzing, whirring sound. He waited. No response. He leaned down and peeked through the lace curtains covering the glass panels at each side of the door. No movement inside the house. Cole frowned and rang the bell again. This time he heard a voice, but couldn't make out the words.

He tried the doorknob, found it unlocked, and opened the door a crack. "Josie?"

"Come in. I'll just be a minute," her voice floated down from upstairs.

He walked into the foyer and closed the door. The hardwoods had a fresh shine and a lemon scent tickled his nose. Josie must have done the floors. Not wanting to track them up, he stayed on the rug, a little surprised she hadn't spent the morning at the office.

"Coming. I'm sorry I'm late."

She turned the corner on the stairs and came into view, then rushed down the final flight, hurrying to meet him. Cole's voice lodged in his throat. She looked wonderful in a sleeveless white, button-up shirt, tied at the waist, and a pair of jeans that fit her like a second skin. Her hair tumbled around her shoulders in the shiny, bouncing curls he remembered from when they were younger. She'd pulled part of it back on top and secured it at her crown with a barrette.

"I got this insane notion to — *Awww!*"

She'd no sooner put one foot onto the foyer floor than it flew out from under her. Cole lunged to catch her, roses flying into the air around them, but met the same fate she did. They both lay sprawled on the floor in a heap at the bottom of the stairs.

"Are you all right?" he asked.

"Oh . . ." she groaned and rubbed her backside.

The feel of her against his chest canceled out the ache in his twisted knee. He couldn't resist trailing a hand down her back. "I know what you mean. Cleaned the floors this morning, *huh?*"

Josie nodded and wiggled herself up into a sitting position. She leaned against the square newel post at the base of the stairs.

Cole propped himself on one arm. "What'd you use?"

"Furniture polish."

He laughed — unable to help himself. Furniture polish!

She arched a brow. "What's so funny?"

"I — I'm sorry." He squeezed her arm. "Honey, you can't clean wood floors with furniture polish."

"Why not?" she frowned. "You clean wood furniture with it."

"Yeah, but you don't have to walk on furniture. And after what just happened, I guess you got your answer."

Her face turned crimson, and she glanced away from him.

He worked himself into a seated position as well and scooted up next to her. "Hey now," he dipped his head until he could see her eyes, "you didn't know."

She crossed her arms. "I really hate being inept."

"You never learned. There's no shame in that."

Clearly she'd put a lot of time and effort into this. He offered a peace token. "Sure put a nice shine on these old heart pine boards."

She threw up her hands in disgust. "What am I going to do about this?"

"For now, you'll just have to avoid this area. The wood'll absorb most of the polish in a few days. I'll show you how to clean 'em then."

She picked up a rose petal from the floor. "Were these for me?"

The flowers he'd brought for Josie were scattered across the floor around them. "Oh, yeah. Here, I'll get 'em."

After a little slipping and sliding on all fours, he gathered all the roses. They were a bit worse for the wear, but he handed them to her anyway.

She buried her face in the damaged bouquet and inhaled. "They're beautiful. Thank you."

"They're nothin' compared to you." He ran his fingers through the hair spilling over her shoulder, loving its silky texture and the way it curled around his fingers. "You look real pretty, Josie Lee."

She rubbed a hand down the leg of her jeans. "It's been a long time since I wore these. I think I've put on a few pounds."

He wiggled his eyebrows. "In all the right places, if you ask me."

She smiled, too, and touched his face. "You certainly know how to flatter a girl, Mr. Craig."

"*Aw,* shucks ma'am. Weren't nothin'. A pretty girl like you probably gets plenty of compliments."

She continued to caress his cheek. "I like yours particularly well."

"I'm happy to oblige."

He touched her hand and pressed a kiss into her palm.

They sat there for several moments, just staring at each other. All kinds of wild fantasies involving them in a tangle on the floor of Josie's foyer about had control of him when she finally said, "So, do you think we can get out of here without breaking something vital?"

"We can give it a try."

"It's a long way to the kitchen and the

back door . . . down that hall." She tipped her head toward the hallway beside the stairs.

"Glad I wore rubber sole shoes."

"That didn't keep you from falling a minute ago."

"Forewarned is forearmed. I'll be more careful this time."

She glanced at her sandals. "I don't think these are going to do so well."

"Here," he reached down and worked the buckle at her slim ankle. "Just slip 'em off." He caressed the bottom of her foot as he helped her remove the strappy, flat sandals.

Josie giggled.

"Ticklish?"

"Very."

He removed the other sandal. This time, he made sure to caress the top of her foot, but in the end, couldn't resist tickling her pink tipped toes.

She giggled again. "Stop that."

"Sorry," he said despite the fact that he was totally unrepentant. "Couldn't help myself."

She didn't look at all upset. In fact, a very becoming blush heightened the color in her cheeks and made him want to spend a few more minutes on the floor exploring other parts of her. But instead, he stood and handed her shoes to her, then helped her up.

When she looked steady on her feet, he asked, "You all right?"

Josie nodded.

"You didn't hurt yourself when you fell now, did you?"

"No, I'm fine. What about you?"

"I'm good to go." With a hand supporting her forearm, he wrapped his other arm around her waist and pulled her close. She put an arm around him, too. They carefully made their way down the hallway that stretched out beside the stairs. Cole couldn't help thinking how nice Josie fit against him. When they finally made it to the kitchen, he was reluctant to let her go.

"That wasn't so bad," she said.

"Not bad at all," he agreed with a wink.

She turned in his arms and said, "I'm beginning to believe you have a one-track mind."

He settled his hands at her waist for a moment, then relished the feel of sliding them around to her back and pulling her up snug against his chest. "How's a man supposed to think about anything but kissing when you're standing this close to him?"

She rested a hand on his chest and looked

up at him beneath long, long red-gold eye-lashes.

"You've been thinking about that, too?" she asked tentatively.

He eased his hand up her back and sank it into the thick curtain of hair falling down her back. "So, you liked my method of getting to know you better last night?"

She frowned. "Yes, but like you said, things aren't always so clear when I'm this close to you." She danced out of his arms and sidestepped her way to the sink. "And we agreed to take things slow."

She retrieved a vase from a cabinet under the sink and filled it with water.

"Did we?"

She glanced over her shoulder and gave him a look, then turned back to shut the water off. Setting the vase on the counter, she arranged the flowers in it.

He touched her arm. When her eyes met his, he said, "I thought we settled this last night."

She rested a hip against the counter. "I did some thinking after you left."

"That sounds serious," he said cautiously. He leaned against the counter, too, but didn't touch her despite the fact that he wanted to with everything in him.

"Can I be honest?"

"Sure."

She ran her fingers along the roses' soft petals, moved a couple of the blooms around until she got the arrangement the way she wanted it . . . which also effectively delayed saying what was on her mind.

"What is it, Josie?"

She darted a glance at him, then refocused on the roses. "This is a little embarrassing."

"You wanna sit?"

"No."

She still hesitated. "Come on, Josie. Don't be shy, now. You can tell me anything."

"Okay." She stared straight ahead, looking out the kitchen window into the backyard. "The fact is, I don't really know how this is supposed to work, and it's possible that I overreacted last night."

One thing at a time. "I'm not sure what you mean. How what's supposed to work?"

"This." She made a motion with her hand, waving it back and forth between them.

"You mean, you and me?"

"Yes."

"I still don't understand."

"Well, I've never really been out with anyone like you."

Cole frowned. "Is that good or bad?"

"Oh, no Cole. I didn't mean it in a bad

way. It's just — Oh, I'm making a mess of this."

She twisted a curl around her index finger.

He couldn't stand it any longer. He gently touched her arms. "Just say what's on your mind. I'm sure we can work through this. Whatever it is."

"The fact is, the men I've dated in the past have been very formal in the way they treated me. Proper."

"You don't think I'm treating you properly?" This was going from bad to worse. Their conversations had a habit of doing that lately.

"No, it's not that. It's me. I don't know how to act, because with other men, I never felt the things that I feel when you touch me and . . . kiss me."

"Oh." He smiled. She had feelings for him. She couldn't have made him happier if she'd told him she loved him.

"Do you understand?"

"I think so. You're saying that you've never been involved with someone you have strong feelings for, and you don't know how things should go."

She let out a breath and smiled. "Exactly."

"Well, then, that's easy. Things between us will go exactly the way you want them to."

"They will?" she asked, still smiling that smile that punched him right in the gut every time.

He nodded. "You set the pace. If you want to talk, we'll talk. If you want to just hang out, we'll hang out. And if you want to kiss," he took a step forward and touched her cheek, "we'll kiss. You know, kissing is a natural part of a relationship."

She had the longest lashes he'd ever seen.

"Is that what this is? A relationship?"

"If that's what you want."

"I'm not sure." She played with a button on his shirt. "The timing is all wrong."

"Why? The computer problem is worked out."

"Yes, but there's so much work to be done. Dealing with the problems in the program put me behind on so many other things that need to be in place in order for the program to be fully operational. I'm not even sure it will function on those old computers at the library. We need faster processors, bigger hard drives, more memory."

"One day off won't ruin you, Josie. It's Saturday after all. Everybody needs a break."

"I know. You're right. I'm just not used to taking weekends off. Even in school, I worked every day."

"Then I'd say you're overdue. So, let's get going." Cole took her hands and pulled her toward the door. "Those Chicago boys won't wait for us."

She tugged against his hands. "Wait. My sweater and purse are by the front door."

He kept pulling her to the backdoor. "We'll get 'em from the front. Is my denim jacket with your things?"

"Yes."

"Come on, then."

"My shoes."

She hopped on one foot after they'd stepped off the back porch trying to put them on. Cole swept her up into his arms and carried her around the house.

"Cole!"

"You'd better quiet down, unless you want everyone in the neighborhood coming out onto their porches to see what's goin' on over here."

As if on cue, Miss Estelee called out, "Howdy-do!" from her back porch. She paused in watering the red petunias in her window boxes. "Well, goodness me, Josie Lee. Did you hurt yourself?"

Josie blushed again. "No, ma'am."

"Oh . . . well, then. Have a nice day." And with that, she hurried into her house.

Cole could have sworn he heard the old woman giggling.

"Oh, no," Josie practically whimpered.

"I tried to warn you."

Cole continued to the sidewalk and set Josie gently on the front porch steps. After he'd retrieved her purse, sweater, and his jacket, he passed her things to her and said, "Want me to lock it?"

She paused in buckling her sandals and pulled her keys out of her purse. "Would you?"

"My pleasure." After locking up, he walked to where she sat on the steps. Holding out a hand, he said, "Ready?"

Josie put her hand in his and stood. "Ready."

Somehow, Cole got the feeling that one word held a wealth of meaning that went beyond just going out on a Saturday night. Tonight could be the beginning of what might, if he played his cards right, turn into something special between him and the girl of his dreams.

# CHAPTER 6

"Here we are," Cole said.

The truck's wheels crunched against gravel as he parked the truck outside a run-down looking warehouse. The parking area was packed with anything from dilapidated pick-ups to high-end luxury vehicles and everything in between.

"Man, we must be runnin' late," Cole said as he opened his door and hopped down from the truck cab.

He met her on the other side just as she was about to step out herself. He grasped her firmly at the waist and gently set her down in front of him.

"Thanks."

He reached around her and pulled a cooler from behind the seat, then shut the door. Next he lifted two lawn chairs out of the truck bed.

"Can I carry something?" she asked.

"Sure." He handed her the small cooler

and took her hand. "Let's go."

"What's all this for?" she asked indicating the cooler and lawn chairs as they crossed the parking lot.

"You'll see."

Several men had gathered outside the building to smoke. They greeted Cole as if he were a regular.

"How's it goin', fellas?" Cole asked good-naturedly.

"Cain't complain. Cain't complain. Ma'am." A man in bibbed overalls and a T-shirt tipped his John Deere hat to her.

"Hello," Josie said.

"This is some kinda crowd, tonight," Cole said.

"Them Chicago boys outdid theirselves."

"A good haul, *huh?*"

"Yeah, buddy." One of the men commented solemnly.

"Well, I guess we'll see ya'll inside."

Cole guided Josie through a side door. Once inside, she stood for a second letting her eyes adjust to the dim lighting.

"Come on," he urged. "All the good seats are just about taken."

Surely he used the word "seats" loosely. There were some ancient folding chairs set up in the back. Some metal, some with wooden bottoms. Like Cole, most of the folks sitting up front had brought an assortment of lawn furniture. Others had put up handmade signs on a number of chairs that read "reserved."

At the front of the room, there was the most awful tangle of what looked like the biggest garage sale she'd ever seen — times twenty.

"What is this place? A flea market?"

"No. It's an auction house."

"You're kidding."

Cole shook his head. "Here we go." They stopped at a row near the front and he set their chairs up.

"Hi-dee, Cole."

"Hey, Thelma Lou. Charlie."

"How do," Charlie said, then nodded at Josie.

"Hello," Josie said. Thelma Lou? *Good Lord, we've taken a wrong turn and landed in Mayberry.*

"Oh, this here's Josie Allen. Josie, this is Charlie and Thelma Lou."

"How do you do," Josie said.

"I do just fine, thanks," the man named Charlie said.

"Looks like a good spread," Cole commented, tipping his head toward the assembled junk.

"Oh sure," Charlie agreed. "Better get at

it before they start."

"Yep," Cole agreed.

Josie had no idea what they were talking about. Get at it?

Cole took the cooler from her, set it between the chairs, then grabbed her hand and said, "Come on."

"Where are we going? I thought we were late."

"We gotta get signed in and check everything out."

"Oh. Okay."

Charlie just shook his head. "First timer?"

"Yeah. But she's a quick learner." To Josie, he said, "Let's go."

He laced his fingers with hers and led her to the front of the room. A lady who sat behind a card table with a clipboard greeted them. "Hey, Cole. Ma'am."

"Hey, Mary Jane."

"You need one or two paddles?"

"Just one."

"Are they for bidding?" Josie asked.

Cole nodded.

Mary Jane smiled. "First timer?"

"Yep." Cole pulled out a credit card and handed it to Mary Jane.

Okay. Josie was getting tired of being talked about as if she weren't there. She was also getting tired of the patronizing comments about her ignorance of how things worked.

"Hope you got plenty of money on this," the lady chuckled around her cigarette, ash falling from the end, as she made an imprint of Cole's card.

Cole laughed, too. "Yep. I'm guessin' she'll be an old hand at it in no time flat." He put his card back in his wallet and handed Josie the paddle. "Here you go."

"Glad to have you, miss," Mary Jane said. To Cole she said, "You better give her a limit."

Had she actually winked at him?

"What was that about?" Josie asked as they walked away.

"Oh, don't think nothin' of it. Just good-natured ribbing. It's her way of welcoming you. You know, she wants you to feel like you fit in."

"Are you saying I don't fit in?"

"No, I just meant it's your first time, and Mary Jane was joking around to make you feel welcome."

Could have fooled her, but she'd keep an open mind. She was out of her element, after all. These people probably wouldn't have any idea how to organize books using the Dewey Decimal System. Well, at least most of them.

"Man . . ." Josie said. They were standing in the middle of the world's biggest garage sale, no doubt about it. Up close, it was almost claustrophobic. Things were stacked up everywhere. Absolutely everything imaginable.

"Don't worry. There's a method to it."

"How could there possibly be?"

"Trust me."

They maneuvered through the narrow pathways that had been left open. Only one person at a time could pass, so she gladly trailed along after Cole. If one of the stacks fell, she could duck behind him. Such a big, muscular man. He could take it. Besides, she couldn't complain about the view. His jeans hugged his hips and thighs in all the right places.

"Just have a look at what's here and make a mental note of the things you'd like to bid on. They'll do the boxes first, then the nick-knacks, pictures and such. They'll work their way up from there to the big items, like the furniture."

Josie nodded, trying to focus.

"See anything you like?"

If he only knew. "Honestly, there's so much, I can hardly assimilate it. One item runs into the next."

"How 'bout this?"

He'd pointed out a nice Victorian table lamp with a marble base and a faded blue, fringe-trimmed shade.

"Pretty," Josie said, "How do you know if it works?"

"You don't."

"Why would you buy something without knowing if it worked?"

"That's half the fun. It's a bonus if it's in perfect working order. If it ain't, lamps are pretty easy to fix."

"Maybe for you."

"I'd fix it for you," he said, leaning down to nuzzle her neck.

Josie giggled. "I'm sure you would. Oh!" She dropped to her knees.

"What?" He went down with her, his hand on her arm. "You okay?"

She just nodded as she poked through a box filled with old, leather-bound books. Running her hand across the smooth spines, she scanned the titles. "Oh my gosh!"

Cole peered over her shoulder. "What?"

"It's *Tom Sawyer.*" She lifted the book out of the box and turned to the copyright page. "Oh my gosh! It's a first edition!"

"*Shh . . .*" he said, glancing around to see if anyone had heard her.

"Do you know how much this is worth?" she whispered.

"I can imagine," he said softly, his breath tickling her ear, "and you'd better keep that kind of information to yourself, unless you want to drive the price up. I mean, there are a few antique dealers here, but they go mostly for the furniture. You could probably get this whole box for five bucks."

She dropped the book. "You're kidding?"

"No, ma'am."

Carefully, she picked it up, examining it to make sure she hadn't damaged it. "Can we just give them five dollars now?"

"No, you have to bid on it."

She reluctantly returned the book to the box. They continued to rummage around until the auctioneer took his place on the raised platform between the seating area and the merchandise.

"We best get our seats," Cole said. "You hungry?"

"A little."

Back at their lawn chairs, Cole flipped open the top on the cooler and said, "I brought canned soft drinks. If you don't like what I have, there's a machine out back."

She took the lemon-lime drink he passed her. "This is fine."

Josie sat back in her chair, her gaze sweeping around the room. What an experience. The whole casual, treasure-hunter atmosphere fascinated her. Some people continued to examine the tangle of items to be sold. Others, like them, relaxed in their chairs, waiting for the auction to begin. Most everyone had brought their own food. Others had gotten hot dogs and popcorn from the concession area in the back. "Interesting."

"What?" He handed her a sandwich wrapped in wax paper.

"This whole scene. It's not at all what I'd expect in an auction."

"The only auctions you've probably ever seen are those high brow affairs where they sell off paintings or rich people's things."

Josie continued scanning the room. "I've never been to an auction period, but I've seen a few on television."

"Yeah. This is *nothin'* like that."

That much, she had surmised. She unwrapped her sandwich, halfway expecting Dixie's chicken salad, but instead found a turkey hoagie.

"Is that okay?" A look of concern creased his brow.

"Yes," she assured him. "I haven't had a hoagie in years." She bit into the sandwich. It tasted wonderful. She set the sandwich on a napkin in her lap and popped the top on her soda. After taking a long drink, she put the can in the cup holder built into the arm of her chair. "That's handy."

"Stick with me and you'll learn all kinds of things I'm sure you never thought you would."

Josie smiled. She had no doubt about that. She took a minute to just stare at Cole. He wore a loose fitting white cotton shirt with a good three buttons undone at his throat revealing a nice view of his smooth, tanned chest. He wore his long hair down today. She liked how he tucked it behind his ears and the way it fell in soft waves past his shoulders.

He wiped his chin with a napkin. "Do I have mustard on my face or something?"

She looked away, trying to smother a smile behind her napkin. "No," she said, then hid behind another bite of her sandwich.

He leaned in close and whispered, "Like what you see?"

Heat rushed up her neck and settled in her cheeks. She swallowed and turned to look at him again. He was so close, they almost bumped noses. The warm, spicy scent of his cologne, combined with his elemental appeal, heightened her desire for him. At length, she managed to say, "Yes."

He tilted his head to the side and kissed her. A brief, intense kiss that left her wanting more. He darted his tongue out to tease the corner of her mouth before breaking the contact. Heat raced through every inch of her body, and she wanted nothing more than to pull him back to her for a more thorough exploration.

"*Mmm.* Mustard tastes so much better that way."

Josie jolted back to reality and wiped her mouth with her paper napkin. Hard to feel sexy when you have condiments dripping down your face.

"Now don't go gettin' all self-conscious," he said as if reading her mind. "Eating can be very sensual."

Josie imagined that watching ice melt with Cole would be sensual. *Hmm* . . . watching ice melt *on* Cole added amazing dimension to the wild fantasies racing through her mind. "Sorry," she said.

"No need to apologize. I enjoyed it."

Josie smiled a secret smile. He thought she'd apologized for having mustard on her face.

The auctioneer pounded his gavel effectively killing the mood. "Let's get started, folks. We got a lot of good merchandise to go through here. The boys really brought some great items down for you tonight."

She leaned toward Cole and whispered.

"Tell me about these Chicago boys. This stuff isn't stolen is it?"

He chuckled. "No. The Chicago boys are really just two guys with a truck who make a run to Chicago every two weeks and bring the goods for the auction back with them."

"Oh."

Three guys who could easily have played the backwoods characters Larry, Darrell and Darrell on the sitcom, *Newhart,* carried boxes to the front of the room.

"They always do the boxes first," Cole said.

"What's in them?"

They both continued to munch on their sandwiches while Larry dug through the contents of the box he held. He pulled out a lace tablecloth, held up some glassware, and a painted vase.

"It's kinda like a grab bag. You never know what you're gonna get. That's ninety percent of the fun."

"Have you ever gotten one?"

"Sure."

"What was in it?"

"Mostly junk."

"Oh." For some reason, she was incredibly disappointed.

"And one of the first Batman comics ever printed, in mint condition."

"Really?"

"Yep."

"Did you sell it?"

"Oh, yeah. Bought a real nice computer with the money I got."

"Wow. Hey, maybe I could get a few computers for the library that way!" she joked.

They'd begun taking bids on the third box. It went for two dollars.

"Can we get one?" she asked a tad breathlessly.

"Sure. Just pick out the one you want and bid."

"How?"

"Listen to the auctioneer. He started the bid on this one at fifty dollars. He always starts high because he gets a percentage of the sells."

Josie listened. The man was saying, "Well give me fifty, give me fifty, give me fifty . . ." Then he went to, "Well give me forty, give me forty, give me forty." He worked it all the way down to ten dollars. When he didn't receive a bid, the man said, a touch of exasperation in his voice, "Somebody start us off."

A person in the front of the room called out, "One dollar."

The auctioneer said, "You're wrong on

this one folks. One dollar, give me two, give me two, who'll give me two?"

Someone near Josie raised his paddle, and the Darrell holding the box called out, "Go!"

Then the auctioneer asked for three. The box finally went for four dollars.

"Think you're gettin' the hang of it?"

She nodded and perched on the edge of her seat to try and see some of the contents of the next box. It had some old annuals, a school letter like you would put on a letter-man jacket, a beat-up football, and some trophies. She'd missed out on high school football games partly because she'd pre-ferred spending her Fridays at the library studying. But Cole had played football. Maybe he might like some of the things in the box.

The bidding started much the same as it had before. She waited until someone called out a bid, then when the auctioneer asked for a higher bid, she raised her paddle. Much to her amazement, no one else bid, and she got the box for two dollars. Win-ning the bid gave her an unexpected feeling of elation. Darrell carried the box over and set it next to Cole.

She leaned across him to peer inside. "Can I go through it now?"

"Let's save it till later. Finish your sandwich."

Josie shook her head and put her hoagie back in the cooler. "I'm too excited to eat."

Charlie sitting down the row from her said, "First timers," under his breath. Mary Lou punched him in the ribs.

*"Ow!"*

"Don't pay him no mind, dear," Thelma Lou said. "You just enjoy yourself."

Josie followed Thelma Lou's advice. She leaned over Cole, her breasts pressed against his arm, to get a better view of the box's contents. "Please? I can't stand it."

He pulled her up by her shoulders, caressed a kiss across her temple and said, "Anticipation makes it much more pleasurable in the end."

Josie grabbed a handful of his soft white shirt and wet her lips with the tip of her tongue. His gaze locked on her mouth like a starving man presented with a smorgasbord.

"Cole?"

"Keep that up, and we'll be out of here in record time."

She wanted to say, "Promise?" but thought that would probably be too forward. Twin desires burned inside her. A need to discover what was in the box, and a need for Cole.

149

She swallowed hard around the knot forming in her throat. The way he watched her made her wonder if he could read her mind.

He slid an arm around her waist and hauled her close to his side.

"Was there anything you were particularly interested in buying?" she asked, tucking a stray strand of hair behind his ear.

"I thought you'd want to bid on that box of books."

"Oh. Yeah." Josie had to work hard to keep the disappointment out of her voice. She missed the mark. Hang the books. She just wanted to be alone with Cole.

"Thank you, God," Cole murmured.

He pointed to the front. Larry was holding the box of books. Cole grabbed the paddle. Somewhat patiently he waited for the bidding to begin. She imagined he didn't want to start the bidding too high. That might tip someone off that there was something valuable inside. In the end, he got the box for ten dollars. Ecstatic, Josie could have jumped up and down, but she restrained herself.

After Larry deposited the box next to the other one, Cole turned to her and said, "Let's get out of here."

"You leavin' already?" Charlie asked in a loud whisper. That drew another sharp elbow to the ribs from Thelma Lou.

"*Ow!*" Charlie complained.

"Ya'll have a nice evenin' now, hear?" Thelma Lou smiled. Her eyes fairly twinkled.

"Goodbye," Josie said, waving. "It was nice to meet you."

Cole stacked the boxes one on top of the other. "Can you get the cooler?"

She nodded.

"I'll come back for the chairs," Cole said.

"Oh, Charlie'll take 'em out, won't you, hon?"

"What? Are you kiddin'?"

That earned him another shot to the ribs. The poor man was going to be black and blue.

He coughed. "I mean, happy to oblige," Charlie said.

The three of them walked out to the truck. After they'd stored everything and thanked Charlie for his help, Cole helped Josie into the truck, and they were on their way.

"Can I look now?" She craned her neck to better see behind the seat where he'd stashed the boxes.

Cole laughed. "So impatient."

"*Uh-huh.* Where are we going? How long will it take to get there?"

He grasped her hand. "Come here."

He pulled her across the bench seat until she sat close enough to touch, her leg pressed against his. It was tricky with the stick shift, but she managed. He put his arm around her, and she snuggled closer. "I'm sure this violates the state seatbelt law."

"I can see you're a play-it-by-the-rules kinda girl."

"Goes with the territory. I am a librarian."

"You don't look like any kinda librarian I've ever seen. Not tonight."

Josie smiled at the compliment. She liked that he thought she was . . . whatever he thought she was. "Are you sorry we didn't stay?"

"Are you?" He glanced at her out of the corner of his eye.

"No, I can't wait to go through the boxes."

His sigh was heavy. "And here I thought we left early because you wanted to be alone with me."

Josie snuggled even closer against his side. "Well, there is that," she said as she pressed a kiss to his neck.

# CHAPTER 7

Cole turned down a gravel road at the edge of town that curved up into the tall pines. The name of it was Pine Lane, but most just called it Lovers' Lane. He gave Josie a sideways look, wondering if she'd comment about him taking her up to the Lovers' Clearing. She didn't say a thing. In fact, she looked anxious. That pleased him immensely.

When they reached the clearing, he put the truck in park and killed the engine. He got out and helped Josie down, then pulled the red plaid blanket they'd used for their lunch date earlier in the week — minus the mess — from behind the seat.

"I'll do that, you get the boxes," Josie took the blanket from Cole, grabbed her sweater, and headed to the center of the clearing.

So much for hoping she'd want to skip the boxes and just make out. "Did anybody ever tell *you* that you got a one-track mind when it comes to books?"

"Sorry," she said. She worked at sounding apologetic, but failed miserably.

He just chuckled. When he'd gathered the boxes, he joined her on the blanket. "Here you go. Which one do you want to go through first?"

"The books."

"How did I know?" He set the box in front of her and said, "Go for it."

She raised up on her knees, but instead of digging into the box, leaned across it and took his face in her hands. She kissed him, a gentle pressure against his lips that ended almost as soon as it began.

"Thank you," she whispered. Then dove into the box.

Cole propped an arm on his bent knee. He rubbed his tingling lower lip with his thumb. He just watched her. The late afternoon sun bathed her in golden splendor. She took his breath away.

"Look! More Mark Twain."

He leaned forward and peered into the box. "How many?"

"I don't know. Two. No, three."

"What else?"

"Several books of poetry, some Shakespeare. Fabulous."

The scene rocketed him back, and he

154

again found himself wishing she'd look at him the way she was eying those books. Just like old times.

"What about this one?" He tapped the other box that contained the old football and trophies.

She shifted her focus. "Didn't you play football?"

He took the ball from her, tossed it into the air, then caught it. "I made the Varsity my sophomore year."

"Did you letter?"

"Naw. I was second string."

"Well, here. Now you have. Hey, it's even from our old *alma mater,* Houston High."

"No kiddin'?"

"Look at this annual."

"How old is it?"

"Wow, it's dated 1962."

She flipped open the book in her hand. The binding crackled with the effort. A musty smell filled the air around them. "The owner's name was Charlie Craig."

"Come on."

"See for yourself." She handed him the annual. "Do you think you're related?"

"Probably a cousin." He flipped to the ads in the back and read an inscription:

"Charlie,

*You're a great guy and a pretty good football*

*player. Have a great summer. Hope we have some classes together next year. Judy.*

"Don't you hate those things?" Josie said.

Cole just shrugged. "I think it's kinda nice." The truth was, he'd never had an annual. His parents hadn't been able to afford one, and he couldn't see spending the money he made from his paper route on anything that wasn't necessary.

"Oh, look. An old wooden box."

She lifted it out, pushed the cardboard box aside, and set it carefully on the blanket between them.

"Looks like a man's jewelry box."

She glanced up at him. A light danced in her eyes. "Really?"

"Open it up and see what's inside."

She tucked her hair behind her ears and carefully raised the lid to the old oak box. It was lined in worn green velvet. Several items sat in the compartments of a divided tray. "Look. Medals."

Cole examined them. "They're for track."

"The two of you had more than a name in common. You were both good athletes. Can't say much for his taste in cufflinks."

She held up a pair with black and white cows on a green enamel background. "Whoa. Must have gotten those in 4-H."

"Or Future Dairymen of America."

156

They both laughed. She lifted the tray and looked underneath. "Oh, Cole . . ." she breathed.

"What is it?"

She held up a tarnished chain with a medallion hanging from it. "It's a senior key."

He swallowed hard.

She delved back inside. "And a class ring." She lifted it out and turned it so she could look at the inside of the ring. "I just realized something."

"What?"

"His initials were C.C."

"So?"

"The same as yours. Hold out your hand."

"Why?"

She grabbed his right hand and before he figured out her intent, she'd slipped it onto his finger. "It fits!"

Cole looked down at the gold ring. Its red stone twinkled back at him. A knot formed somewhere in the region of his gut.

"What's wrong?" She squeezed his hand until he looked at her. "Cole?"

"It's nothing."

She laced her fingers with his. "Tell me."

He lifted one shoulder, then admitted, "It's stupid."

"Come on. You told me I could tell you

anything. Now, it's your turn."

"It just brings back old memories. Some, not so good."

"Memories of your dad's illness?"

"Yeah. That and . . . other things." Memories of a young girl he'd wanted to get to know, but who'd always been out of his reach.

"You missed out on high school." She paused, then added, "You were pretty popular. Good at sports, too. You may have gotten an athletic scholarship if . . ."

"If Dad hadn't got sick?"

Josie nodded.

Cole hadn't thought about that time in his life for years. He didn't particularly want to rehash it now, but she wouldn't let it go.

"Did he ever get any better?"

"He recovered, but the doctor said he'd never be able to do hard labor again."

"How is he now?"

"He died a couple of years back."

Josie squeezed his hand again. "I'm sorry. I didn't know. He was a good man, Cole."

"Thanks."

"What about your mom. How is she?"

He nodded. "Doin' great. She moved to Maryville a few years back to live with her sister. I'm gone so much of the time, I guess she got lonely. Aunt Shirley has a condo in

158

one of those retirement communities."

He regretted the words as soon as they left his mouth.

"So you're all alone out on your farm now?"

"Yep."

She quieted for a moment, and he figured she was about to ask him why he would say he was gone most of the time. But instead, she asked, "What would you have done?"

"What do you mean?"

"If you hadn't had to quit school, what would you have done? What were your goals? What did you dream of becoming?"

Her question hit a little close to home. He didn't want to get into any of this right now. It was too soon.

"I don't know. Doesn't really matter. A body can't go back and change things, and there's no use wonderin' what might have been."

"But it doesn't have to be about what might have been. Tonight, it could be about dreaming a little." She looked up at him, a starry look shining in her pretty eyes. "Don't you ever dream, Cole?"

Seemed he'd been dreaming about her most of his life. He wondered what she'd say if he told her that.

"What's that grin about?" she asked.

"Memories. They weren't all bad."

"Tell me," she encouraged softly.

"Well, you know, I was only sixteen when dad . . . when he had his first heart attack. I was just finishing my sophomore year. I didn't have any big plans for the future. My goals were more immediate."

"Like what?"

"I was looking forward to you moving up to the high school in the fall."

"You were?"

He nodded slowly, watching for her reaction.

"Why?"

"I planned on asking you to the homecoming dance, and the junior-senior prom."

"Me?" she asked. The word came out as a high-pitched squeak. "Why?"

He hadn't expected that question. "You don't believe me?"

"I'm wondering what kind of an impression a sixth grader with no social skills could make on an eighth grader."

He brushed the backs of his fingers against her cheeks. "Even then, there was just something about you. Something special and intriguing."

She shook her head. "There was no intrigue. I didn't have friends because I didn't fit in."

"There was that, too. You always seemed lonely to me."

Her laugh sounded false and nervous. "It may have seemed that way when we were in middle school, but after you moved up to the high school —"

"Nothing changed. Come on, Josie, I saw you. With the schools side by side, I saw you ever now and then. You still sat by yourself at recess and read." He paused before continuing. "I wanted to get to know you. Keep you company. Talk about the books you loved so much."

"Why didn't you?"

He laughed. Time to lighten things up a little. "Boys were supposed to play at recess. Not read. I had my rep to consider."

She pushed at his shoulder and he fell backwards against the blanket. He propped himself up on one arm.

"Were you really going to ask me to the homecoming dance?"

"Yep." He looked down at the heavy, unfamiliar ring on his finger. "I would have gotten one of these my junior year. I'd been savin' up for it."

Josie stretched out beside him on the blanket and ran her index finger around the stone in the ring, but she didn't speak. He tipped her chin up until their eyes met. A sudden sadness filled her golden gaze. "Hey, what's wrong?"

She shook her head. "I was just thinking about how our lives might have been different. You know, if you hadn't been forced to quit school."

He cradled her warm, soft cheek in his hand. "You would have still been valedictorian."

"Maybe."

"For sure. You'd probably have just seen me as a dumb jock."

"I doubt that. Those boys who used to call you that awful name, they were the stupid ones. I bet between them, they didn't have a 2.0."

He laughed at her characterization of them. Her hair fell across her shoulder to the blanket. He couldn't resist testing its texture. It felt soft and silky as it glided through his fingers. He remembered again the time she'd tripped that boy in Town Square who'd been calling him "coal bucket." She must have been about fifteen. A freshman in high school. But by then, he'd already dropped out.

A silence ensued. She rolled onto her stomach and pulled up some grass, then let it fall through her fingers. "I have a confession."

"What's that?"

"I thought you were pretty cute back then. I guess I had a little crush on you after you rescued me from Bobby Jones."

"Seems I was destined to be your knight." He sat up. "Come here."

She pushed herself up and scooted over until he could pull her close. With her back pressed against his chest, he wrapped his arms around her waist.

"What about now?" He teased her temple with a kiss. "Still think I'm cute?"

She nodded.

"So, you had a secret crush on me." That tidbit of information surprised him. "I never would have thought you noticed anything outside the pages of those books you read."

She sat straighter and said, "I noticed a lot of things. Who knows, if you had still been at the high school when I got there, maybe we would have dated."

"I doubt it."

She looked back at him. "What makes you say that?"

"Come on, Josie." He tried to pull her back into his arms, but she resisted. He sighed. "You know your folks wouldn't have allowed it."

"Why not?"

"Like I said, no use wastin' time on 'what

163

ifs'. I've done okay for myself."

Looking into her wide, trusting eyes, he felt more than a twinge of guilt for the game he was playing. But if he told her the truth now, when she seemed ready to give them a chance . . . He just couldn't risk messing it all up. Not now.

"No. I want to know. Why do you think my parents wouldn't have allowed me to see you?"

"You know why, Josie."

She turned back around. Her head fit nice against his shoulder.

"I guess I know what you're thinking. That they wouldn't allow their little princess of the Ridge to date someone from the back side of town, right?"

She was getting defensive.

"You sayin' I'm wrong?"

"Yes. My parents weren't like that, Cole."

He didn't like the direction this conversation was taking. He stood and walked away a few paces.

Josie followed. "You don't believe me, do you?"

"There's no point in this. We can't rewrite history."

She took in their surroundings. "Everyone says this place, this clearing in the tall pines, is magical. I've heard stories about it all my life. That this is where the angels live. That they bless the very ground we're standing on." She spun back to face him. "I heard someone say the stars up here come down so close that they almost touch the ground."

"I never took you for the fanciful type, Josie Lee."

She shrugged and looked away. "I always wondered about it. No one ever brought me here, so I guess I just let my imagination take flight."

He ran his hands from her shoulders to her wrists. "I would've brought you here."

She cast him a sideways look. "I only saw you a couple of times after you left school."

"I tried to keep my distance."

"Why?"

"Come on, Josie, you know that my payin' you the least bit of attention wouldn't have gone unnoticed. And then there was the fact that you were so young, and I was a drop-out."

"You couldn't help that. I wouldn't have looked at you that way."

"That's easy to say now, when you don't really have to make the choice."

She shoved her hands into the back pockets of her jeans and raised her chin a notch. "You don't give me enough credit. And while we're on the subject, can I just say that I get really tired of having to live up to what people expect of me? I wish . . ."

"What?"

She crossed her arms and said a little defiantly, "I wish I could just be plain old Josie."

He rubbed his chin. "And how is plain old Josie different from the Josie who was valedictorian and is now Dr. Allen?"

"Let's just say, for starters, that I don't really subscribe to the code of conduct expected of a librarian."

"Is there a for instance in there?"

"Like being a member of the Association of University Women. I'd rather watch grass grow."

Cole thought she'd probably fit right in with that group, but he asked, "What would you rather do?"

She walked back to the blanket, sat, pulled her knees up to her chest and started rocking back and forth. Cole followed.

"I have dreams just like anyone else."

He could almost see the excitement pulse through her. She chanced a look at him.

"I've always wanted to own a little shop where I could sell old and rare books. Kind of like the ones we found in that box. A place where you could sit and drink coffee or hot tea and enjoy a good read."

He stood looking down at her. "So what's stoppin' you?"

She focused on a spot across the clearing. It was as if someone had turned a light off inside her. "Mrs. McKay wouldn't approve. She expects me to live, breathe, and sleep the library."

He dropped down beside her. "Are you sayin' you wish you could be something other than the town librarian?"

"Oh, no. I've wanted to be a librarian since I was a little girl."

"But you want more."

She nodded.

"So, what are you going to do about it?"

She shrugged. "What can I do?"

"Mrs. McKay and this town don't own you, Josie Lee."

Her laugh was harsh. "You have no idea. What about you? Are you happy being the town's handyman?"

He paused, considering his response. "Keeps life simple when you live up to people's expectations."

"Sure. But does it make you happy?"

He scooted across the blanket so that he could bump her arm with his. "You make me happy."

Her smile was a slice of pure heaven.

"I have an idea," he said. "For the rest of

the evening, let's forget Mrs. McKay and the town's expectations and just be ourselves."

"Sounds good," she said. "Let's let this place work its magic. Let's turn back time and pretend we're both simple high school students."

He slid his arm around her waist. "Come here." He pulled her over so that she sat between his legs. She leaned back against his chest, resting her head on his shoulder as she looked up at the sky. A beautiful East Tennessee sunset painted it all blues, purples, and grays with a brilliant flash of red-orange.

"So, are you going to keep it?" she asked.

"What?"

She lifted his hand from her waist. "The ring."

He looked at the class ring, then back at her. "Not if I can help it."

Josie frowned. "I don't see why not." She traced the faceted cuts of the stone with the tip of her fingernail. "You said you always wanted one."

"True, but you know, it's customary for a guy to give his class ring to his girl."

Her frown cleared. "Oh." She turned back to the sunset, leaning against his chest again.

Cole hesitated. He felt just like a teenager.

All nervous and uncertain. The girl of his dreams finally seemed within his reach, but just like in young love, one wrong move, and it could all be over. Still, maybe they *could* go back in time. Pretend she wasn't the town's golden girl, and he wasn't just a Craig from the wrong side of the ridge, even if it was just for tonight.

He circled her waist with his arms and removed the class ring from his finger. Holding it in front of her, he took a deep breath. *Just go for it.*

"Josie Lee Allen, will you be my girl?"

# CHAPTER 8

Josie touched the ring, then pulled her hand back, almost afraid she was dreaming. When she was young, she'd played a scene just like this out in her mind hundreds of times.

Of course, no one had ever given her their class ring. She'd never had a boyfriend, or a date to a dance. She'd been uncomfortable around boys in high school. In college, she hadn't found anyone she wanted to be with beyond a casual date. Even though she'd been mildly curious about moving past goodnight kisses, that's all it had been. Curiosity.

But now, things were different. Cole cared about her. And when he kissed her, her thoughts went light years beyond curiosity.

She touched the ring again, took it and held it. The warmth left from his fingers seeped into hers. She turned in his arms. The dusky light of that time between day and night gave his hair a silvery cast, his face a chiseled look highlighted by light and shadow. He again reminded her of the handsome sword-bearing warrior depicted in the town's angel monument. He looked just like an archangel come down from heaven.

"You want me to be your girl?"

He pushed her hair away from her face with gentle hands. "Always," he whispered. "I've always wanted you."

Her heart swelled at his words and she let the fantasy take hold. "Can I tell you a secret?"

He nodded.

"I've always dreamed of finding someone who would want me. Someone who'd love me just for me, the person I really am. Not the person people expect me to be."

He trailed his fingertips up her cheek. "Let me be that someone."

Had she waited to hear someone say that most of her life? Suddenly, it felt that way. She circled his neck with her hands and kissed him. She longed to show him how she felt, but Cole surprised her by pulling back.

"What's wrong?" she asked.

"First things first. You haven't given me an answer yet."

He removed her hands from his neck and grasped her wrist. The gold ring she held between them sparkled with a life of its own. For now, she'd pretend it had magical properties that would bind them together when they went back to the real world.

"I'd be honored," she said.

The smile on his face could have lit up the entire city. He slid the ring onto her index finger, but the too large size and weight of the stone caused it to spin toward her palm.

"I have an idea. Where's that senior key you found?" he asked.

Josie reached over and pulled the key with its long, tarnished gold chain out of the jewelry box and handed it to Cole. Taking it, he put the ring on the chain, then secured it around her neck. He lifted her hair so that it wasn't caught inside the chain.

"There. Perfect," he said.

The ring and key nestled against her breast, near her heart. She clasped it in her hand. The comfort of its weight and warmth felt real. Confirmed that this wasn't a dream.

She touched his face, traced his high cheekbones with her fingertips. "I couldn't agree more. Now, can we kiss?"

"Absolutely." He sank his fingers into her hair and slowly pulled her forward.

Before he kissed her, she felt a warm

gentle breeze. Too warm for a springtime evening on the ridge, but it seemed to heighten her awareness of everything. Cole's hand on her face, his arm around her waist, her anticipation in kissing him. . . .

Their lips met and the sensation was nothing short of electric. It sounded cliché. They'd kissed before, but those kisses couldn't compare to this. This time, there was a connection. A oneness in the experience.

Josie wrapped her arms around Cole and held on tight. She wanted the feeling to go on forever. It was like they were wrapped in a cocoon. Like nothing in the universe existed outside this moment and these intense feelings swirling around them, so that she didn't know where she ended and he began.

When he at last lifted his lips from hers, she opened her eyes with reluctance. What she saw when she looked into his beautiful eyes reflected what she felt.

"Whoa."

"Did you feel that?" she whispered. She was afraid if she spoke too loudly, the spell might be broken.

"Oh, yeah." Cole continued in hushed tones as well.

"The other times — I mean — the other

kisses —"

"I know."

An almost eerie quiet blanketed the clearing. No night sounds filled the air. No crickets, no tree frogs, nothing but utter silence.

Cole pressed his mouth to her neck. He began a painstaking exploration of every inch of exposed skin from her chin to the bend of her shoulder. Being here with him like this felt like the most natural thing in the world. She wanted everything at once. To know all his secrets, to see inside his heart. She rested her hand on his chest. The strong reassuring beat she felt beneath her palm served as another reassurance that this was real rather than a dream.

He eased her down to the blanket. She pushed his hair back from his face as he slid a hand over her hip to her thigh. The feelings rocking her intensified, if that were possible. She felt ultra-sensitized to his touch, his kiss.

She slipped her hand inside the collar of his shirt and quickly became annoyed when a button halted the downward progress of her hand along the warm, hard, satin smoothness of his chest. She undid one button, two, then three. His teeth scraped the skin of her neck and chin before he plunged his tongue into her mouth, completely possessing her with his kiss.

He slid his knee between hers and she bent her leg until she'd nestled his hip against her thigh. Her shirt must have ridden up in the back, because his hand was against the small of her back and moving inside the waist of her jeans. Josie arched her back. Cole moaned his pleasure into the kiss.

"Cole —"

"Josie —"

They'd both spoken at the same time. Their names, though a mingled whisper, filled the clearing and echoed in the silent night until the sound merged and settled in the tall pines that seemed to reach straight up to heaven. Suddenly, the crickets began to chirp again. The tree frogs continued their song of coming summer.

Cole and Josie just looked at each other. She didn't know what to say. Didn't have the words to explain what had just happened. Still, something new and strange burned inside her so that it filled her heart almost to bursting with feeling for him.

He sat up and pushed the hair back from his face. She followed and wrapped her arms around one of his. She couldn't stand to be separated from him.

"Josie, I'm sorry. I don't know what happened just now. I didn't mean to be disrespectful. I care about you."

"*Shh . . .*" She pressed her fingertips to his lips. "I know. Just hold me."

Sheltered in the warmth of his embrace, Josie knew that she would be linked to Cole Craig for the rest of her life. She hadn't planned on this happening when she'd returned to Angel Ridge. Books were her life. Relationships, foreign territory. But wrapped in his strong arms here in the Lovers' Clearing surrounded by the magical tall pines, she felt safe in exploring what a new life with someone like him could offer.

She wasn't kidding herself. The problems of a relationship between them still existed. Maybe they could live out the fantasy, at least for the rest of the weekend. But come Monday morning, she'd have to figure out a way to deal with Mrs. McKay.

Cole entered the First Baptist Church of Angel Ridge to discover the back pews already filled. He checked his watch. Right about time for services to begin. Had to get to church early to get a good seat in the back. He smiled. Some things never changed.

He scanned the back rows, looking for

Josie. She sat on a pew to his left that was filled to capacity. All prim and proper in a dark blazer, she'd pulled her pretty hair into that tight knot that he hated. As if she sensed that someone was staring at her, she turned and their gazes locked, but she looked away almost as soon as she saw him. What was that all about?

*"Psst."*

Dixie Ferguson, who sat on the opposite side of the church, was shoving her brother, Blake, over to make room for one more. How could he have missed Dixie? She was wearing a bright red hat that matched the large flowers printing her painfully yellow dress. He walked over to join them.

The astute Dixie wasted no time. "So, what's put that nice color in your cheeks?"

He just shrugged. "Hey, Dix. You look bright. How's it goin', Blake?"

"No complaints," Blake replied.

"Well, I'll take your lack of response as the male code of 'don't kiss and tell.' "

"Give the man a break, Dix," Blake said.

She swung her brother "a look," then said, "Well, since you haven't told me what to do in, well, ever, big brother, I'll just ignore that, especially since I am a grown woman *with* a mind of my own." She rolled her eyes and returned her attention to Cole. "So, did you take her out yesterday?"

No need in denying it. She'd pry it out of him eventually. "Yeah," he confirmed.

She nudged him with her elbow. Man, what was it with women and elbows anyway?

"And it went well?"

Cole rubbed his ribs. "I thought so." He looked over his shoulder at Josie. She gave him a little smile this time before breaking eye contact. That was encouraging.

Dixie frowned. "What do you mean, 'thought so'?"

"She didn't save me a seat."

"Did you ask her to?"

"No."

"Well, then you should have gotten here sooner and claimed your place."

"I had a few things to take care of."

"Havin' to work on a Sunday?" Blake asked.

"What would Pastor Strong say?" Dixie added.

Cole just shrugged. He noticed that Blake nodded his understanding. Blake was probably the only person in town that knew his secret. The fact was, all the time he'd been spending in town the past couple of weeks, looking for opportunities to spend time with Josie, had put him behind on a couple of projects that were deadlining. Which brought him to another reality. If he and Josie were going to have something, that something couldn't get started on a ground littered with secrets and half-truths. He had to tell her everything. The sooner the better.

He chanced another look back at her. She was beautiful even with her hair pulled back like that. She was even more beautiful today. Had a kind of glow about her.

Last night had been amazing. Holding her and kissing her had been like nothing he'd ever experienced. He'd heard about all those romantic notions of mystical things happening when you were with "the one," but he never would have believed it to be real. Not until last night.

"Oh, there's Miss Estelee." Dixie nudged him again. "Don't she look nice in that pretty blue hat?"

Cole and Blake shared a look. Women. "Real nice color," Cole agreed, because it was expected. He'd never understood the rapid topic shifts women seemed to enjoy, or the fashion commentary. He probably wouldn't have even noticed Miss Estelee's hat if Dixie hadn't pointed it out.

Unlike Dixie, Miss Estelee wore much more subdued colors. Now that he thought of it, Miss Estelee always wore a hat to church. Something she and Dixie had in common.

The choir walked in five minutes late, as usual, and took their spots in the choir loft. While they sang a short, upbeat song to begin the service, Dixie whispered, "You bringin' Josie over to the diner for Sunday lunch?"

"Nope. Thought we'd picnic at the Fort."

She arched a brow. "That's a bold move, takin' her out in front of the whole, entire town. Good for you!"

He frowned. "Whole town? What are you talkin' about, Dix?"

He had to wait for a response while they stood and turned to the appropriate page in the Baptist Hymnal and sang a congregational hymn. He could hardly wait for it to end and the morning announcements to begin. While Pastor Strong recounted what missions group would meet when, and where the seniors would be going this Friday, Cole asked Dixie again. "Somethin' going on at the Fort that I don't know about?"

"Encampment weekend," Dixie whispered. "Supposed to be a beautiful day. They should have a good turn out."

Cole groaned inwardly. The last thing he needed was a crowd. He wanted Josie to himself for more reasons than one. They really needed to have a heart to heart.

Throughout the service, he couldn't help glancing back at Josie. He caught her eye a few more times. He smiled. At least he was on her radar. The service couldn't end too soon for him. Maybe she'd let him give her a ride back to her house.

As luck would have it, Pastor Strong went extra long today. He always got that way when he preached about morality, which was about once a month. As soon as the last notes of the benediction ended, Cole said goodbye to Dixie and Blake, then tried to get to Josie. Everyone crowded into the aisles at once. He couldn't move an inch, but Josie had a clear shot out the side door. Dang it.

"Cole! Cole Craig!"

He turned to find old Mrs. McKay bearing down on him. Great. He took a deep breath and prepared himself.

"Hello, Mrs. McKay," he nodded to the tall, thin woman. "Vistin' the Baptists this morning?"

"Reverend McElroy is ill, so there are no services at First Presbyterian."

"I hadn't heard. Hope it's not anything serious."

"Yes, yes. I have a cold draft in my bedroom."

Cole almost burst out laughing at the woman's abrupt statement. Dixie must have heard, because she had to cough to cover hers. A cold draft in her bedroom. Big surprise. Everybody knew the woman was the coldest fish in town.

When he made no response, Mrs. McKay propped a long, thin hand on her bony hip. "I'd like you to come over and plug it."

Now that was a frightening visual. He shook his head to clear the image. "I'll try to get over by there this week to see — I mean, have a look — Oh —"

"Tomorrow."

"Beg pardon?" He couldn't believe her high and mighty tone, even though he should certainly be used to it by now.

"You'll come by tomorrow."

Mr. DeFoe walked by about then and having heard the command, just shook his head and kept moving, mumbling something under his breath.

"I'll do my best, ma'am." He was purposely non-committal. He'd not be ordered about like a servant. He'd come by that drafty old mansion of hers when he good and well got around to it.

The woman turned on her sturdy heels, and Cole thought he heard her saying,

"Good help is impossible to find these days."

She had no idea. She'd be lucky if he got by there before two weeks passed. Cole turned back toward the exit, still hoping to catch Josie in the parking lot, but he almost walked right over little old Miss Estelee. He had to grab the back of a pew to keep from falling over her.

"Miss Estelee! I'm sorry. I didn't see you standin' there."

"*Tsk, tsk.* That woman. She should treat folks better'n she does."

Surprised, Cole said, "Mrs. McKay? Oh, I don't pay her no mind."

"*Hmm.* Well, that's half the problem. Folks lettin' her get away with it all the time. And in church of all places. Why I can remember when her people didn't have more than two nickels to rub together. Course, she wouldn't know about that. More's the pity. Still, I have a mind to head out of here and give her a piece of my mind."

Cole touched the woman's arm. "Don't trouble yourself about it, Miss Estelee. I won't."

She cackled and tapped his forearm. "You're a good boy, Cole Craig." She leaned in and whispered. "Why, if I was a few years younger, I'd give our young Josie a run for her money."

He laughed. "I'd have a decision on my hands, too. Good thing I don't have to choose. I'm hopin' you'll both be my girls."

Was Miss Estelee . . . blushing? She smoothed the wispy, bluish-white hair framing her face.

"You're a natural born charmer, Cole Craig. Your slick talkin's enough to turn a girl's head. Even a girl my age."

He laughed. "Is there somethin' I can do for you, Miss Estelee?"

"I was hopin' you could give me a ride back to my house."

Cole offered the woman his arm. So much for catching up with Josie. Still, he wondered . . . "Doc Prescott not around this mornin'?" The town doctor usually took lunch with Miss Estelee. It had been a standing date for years. Everyone in town knew about it.

"I think he must have gone out to check on the Reverend McElroy. I'd walk, but my old bones is a creakin' today. There's a cold rain settin' in, I declare."

They'd made their way through the vestibule and out onto the front portico. It was a warm, bright sunshiny day. Not a rain cloud in sight, but he humored the old lady. "Could be. I'd be happy to drive you home, ma'am." He had to pick Josie up for their date anyway. Date. He liked the sound of that.

Miss Estelee patted his arm. "There's a good boy. I do appreciate it."

"My pleasure, ma'am," he said. But as they approached his truck, he wondered how he'd help the old, diminutive woman up into the cab.

"Oh, you brought your hound."

A sleepy Rick raised his head and thumped his tail against the truck bed. Cole unlocked the passenger door and opened it. "Josie and I are going to the Fort for a picnic. I thought I'd bring him along."

"Oh, he's a dandy."

"That's kind of you to say, Miss Estelee, but he's about worthless. Just lays around and sleeps all day."

"Well, of course he does. He's a hound dog," she declared as if everyone should expect nothing more of such a dog.

"Let me help you up," Cole offered.

"Thank you, dear."

There was nothing for it. Cole grasped the woman by the waist and lifted her up onto the seat.

"Whew! I wasn't expectin' that."

"I'm sorry. Did I hurt you, ma'am?"

Miss Estelee laughed and slapped her

knee. "No, honey. I come from stronger stock than that. Hop in and let's go."

He shut the door and just shook his head as he walked around to the driver's side.

When he was in the truck, he noticed that Miss Estelee's mood had shifted. She had a faraway look in her eyes. "Everything okay, ma'am?" he asked before starting the truck.

She cleared her throat and was slow in responding. Finally, she said, "Drive me by the angel monument, would you, Cole? Drive by real slow. I want to have a good look at him today."

He frowned, puzzled by her words. "Sure thing, Miss Estelee." He started the truck. "The impatiens I put in for you are spreadin' out real nice. I think you'll be pleased."

The old lady just nodded. As they drove by the monument, he could have sworn she teared up, but she didn't say another word until she thanked him for the ride when they arrived at her house.

She looked so sad as she walked up the steps to her front door, Cole asked if she'd like to spend the day with him and Josie. He wouldn't have believed it if he hadn't heard the words coming out of his own mouth. Miss Estelee just shook her head and said she'd enjoy the afternoon alone in front of the fireplace in her parlor.

Seemed a bit warm for a fire, but he didn't press the point. He turned toward Josie's house. An afternoon alone with Josie and half the population of Angel Ridge . . . Maybe he could talk her into a picnic at his place instead.

Josie hurried home after church. She quickly changed out of her dress into a pair of white cotton shorts and a pink tank top she'd bought at Heart's Desire yesterday after she'd cleaned the floors. Cole would be here any minute.

She hadn't gotten much of a head start on him leaving the church. She'd felt bad about not saving him a seat. She'd planned to, but then Mrs. McKay had shown up. She knew she was going to have to deal with the woman sooner or later. This morning, in the crowded church, she'd opted for later. Still, she'd enjoyed the stolen looks they'd shared throughout the service. And he'd be here any minute. She'd better get moving.

She pulled the pins out of her hair and ran a brush through it quickly, then braided it so that it lay in a long line down her back. Grabbing her pink espadrilles and a pink gingham button-up shirt to put on over the tank top, she ran down the back stairway to the kitchen.

She held the class ring that lay between her breasts so the heavy metal wouldn't bounce against her chest as she jogged down the stairs. She hadn't removed it since Cole had put it around her neck last night and didn't plan to. Remembering the way he'd asked her to be his girl brought a smile to her lips. A warmth spread through her when she thought of how they'd kissed. Never in her life had she experienced anything like it. She spun around in a circle when she reached the kitchen. Lord, he was seven kinds of wonderful.

Today, he'd planned another picnic for them. This time at Fort Loudoun. Hopefully it wouldn't be too crowded, but on such a beautiful Sunday afternoon, it would likely be crawling with Angel Ridge residents enjoying the springtime weather. Oh well, no one would probably recognize her out of a business suit with her hair down. But where were her hat and sunglasses, just in case?

Cole knocked on the back door before she'd had time to search for the items. Dang it. She'd taken longer than she should have changing.

"Come in."

"Hey."

Josie glanced over her shoulder at him.

He wore the khaki slacks and blue polo he'd worn to church, and he carried a pair of shorts in his hand. Funny, she hadn't noticed earlier that all the buttons on his shirt had been undone. Her heart did a funny flutter inside her chest then kicked into overdrive.

"Hi." She leaned against the counter and just let her gaze roam from his head to his toes and back again. Gathering the needed items for their picnic would just have to wait.

He walked over to her and without saying another word, put an arm around her waist, pulled her close, and proceeded to kiss any remaining rational thought right out of her head. The shorts he'd been carrying hit the hardwoods so he could free up a hand to slide around her neck.

*"Mmm,"* he said against her lips. "I've wanted to do that all mornin'."

She loved the silky feel of his hair slipping through her fingers. "I'm sure Pastor Strong would be disappointed to hear that, especially since his sermon this morning was on purity of thought."

"Yeah, he was real wound up today. Must have known everyone had plans this afternoon that would likely keep them out of church tonight." He traced the thin line of bare skin at her waist exposed above her shorts. "I wanted to sit with you, but there was no room at all on that pew."

The weight of her guilt broke the mood. Josie stepped out of his arms because she was afraid her eyes would give her away. She stooped to pick up his shorts and laid them on the island. "Well, you know, you have to get there early to get a spot in the back."

He followed her. His arms came around her waist from behind, and he rested his chin on her shoulder. "Save me a seat next time, *huh?*"

"Okay." She was definitely going to hell for lying on a Sunday, but there was no way she'd come clean and tell him she didn't want Mrs. McKay and all of Angel Ridge to see them sitting together in church. Not yet anyway. "I just got here. I don't have the picnic basket packed yet."

"No hurry. You look great, by the way." He repositioned himself so that he could give her a thorough visual examination that left her feeling all warm and tingly. "I don't think I've ever seen this much of your legs." He trailed a hand down her thigh. "Nice."

She sucked in a jagged breath. "You know, it's kind of hard to get anything accomplished when you're doing that."

He still had an arm around her waist and his hand had shifted to the front of her thigh. All the while, he was sprinkling feather-light kisses down the back of her neck.

"Sorry, but you feel so good and you look so beautiful, I can't keep my hands and lips off you."

Hearing those words coming from Cole made her weak. Josie gave up and leaned back against him. She tilted her head to the side and reached up to trail her hand down the back of his head. "Cole . . . I really can't concentrate when you do that."

"Good."

"Cole . . . lunch."

He stepped away with obvious reluctance. "And here I thought I was doin' my best irresistible act. Miss Estelee thought so, anyway. I think she said somethin' about her givin' you a run for your money if she was younger."

Josie laughed. "I'm not even going to ask."

"Guess you must be hungry."

Oh yeah. Standing in her kitchen with him only a touch away, she was hungry all right. In fact, if she didn't get out of this house soon, they'd never make it to the Fort.

"I'm sorry." She touched his face. "Would it help if I said you *are* irresistible?"

191

"Maybe. If you say it with a kiss."

"You're irresistible." She stood on tiptoe and kissed him. A kiss that quickly morphed into a long, thorough exploration. . . .

Some moments later, she broke the contact and looked up into blue eyes that had turned the color of sapphires.

"*Mmm.* Keep that up and we'll be havin' our picnic here."

Tempting, but risky. "No way. You promised me the Fort."

"Yeah, about that. I found out they're havin' an encampment this weekend."

"Really? I haven't been to one of those in years. Do they still have the soldiers in uniform recruiting for the British Regulars?"

"Yep. And the ladies cook stew in big black pots over campfires. I think they still make lye soap, too. In the same pots."

"Yeah, but not at the same time. I can't wait." She pulled a loaf of bread toward her on the counter and worked the twisty tie. When she turned to get the peanut butter out of the cabinet, Cole leaned back against the counter and sighed. He didn't look at all excited. "Something wrong? Don't you want to go?"

"I was lookin' forward to some quiet time with you. It'll be crazy out there."

Lots of people. Maybe they could get lost

in the crowd. This was a good thing, especially if she could come up with that hat and those glasses. She also loved live history reenactments. She tugged at his hand and gave him what she hoped was a pleading look. Problem was, she had no experience in the fine art of cajoling, feminine behavior. "Come on, it'll be fun."

"You sure I couldn't interest you in a picnic on my farm instead?"

She was tempted. Incredibly tempted, but she said, "I'd really like to go out to your farm sometime, but I was looking forward to going to the Fort today. It's been so long since I've been there. And besides, you live so far out."

"Yeah, so?"

"*Umm,* I have to go in to work later."

He frowned. "On a Sunday?"

She spread peanut butter on bread. "I have to revise and print out some reports before tomorrow. I'd rather do it tonight than go in early in the morning."

"You are way too dedicated."

"It's expected."

Cole made no comment about that, but his expression said it all. He watched with interest as she continued spreading peanut butter on bread. "What are you fixin'?"

"You have two choices. Peanut butter and

banana or peanut butter and jelly."

He chuckled. "Which do you recommend?"

"They're both house specialties."

"You know, I could get us some fried chicken from Ferguson's."

She felt inexplicably hurt by the comment, but she should have known a sandwich wouldn't satisfy a man as large as Cole. "I'm sorry."

"Oh no, honey. I'm sorry. I didn't mean to criticize your, *um,* cooking. I love peanut butter and banana sandwiches."

"You don't lie very well, Cole Craig."

"Well, maybe if you add some mayonnaise."

Mayonnaise? Disgusting. She turned and put the knife in the sink. "I'm sorry I can't cook."

He took her in his arms and said, "You think I care that you can't cook?"

She picked a piece of lint off his shirt. "You probably will in the long run."

He tipped her chin up until her gaze met his. He wore a big, silly grin. "There's gonna be a long run?"

She certainly hoped so, but she wasn't ready to say the words. Not yet. So, she gave him a playful smack on the chest. "Why don't you go change while I finish packing lunch? Bathroom's through there."

"Okay. If you're sure I can't talk you into a picnic at the farm. There's a real nice spot by the creek that you'd love."

"Another time?"

His sigh sounded heartfelt. "I'll hold you to it." Picking up his shorts, he leaned down to kiss her cheek. "The Fort it is."

When he'd disappeared into the bathroom, Josie turned her attention back to packing food into the basket. The Fort it was. Lots of people. Now, where had she put that straw hat with the really wide brim? Maybe she'd left it out on the sun porch. . . .

# CHAPTER 9

They had to park a quarter of a mile from the entrance to the Fort. Cole sighed. When he looked over at Josie, she sat on the edge of her seat looking beautiful and like she could hardly wait for them to find a parking space. He wished he could work up the same kind of enthusiasm. Even Rick was dancing around in the truck bed, and he didn't get excited about much of anything. So much for loyalty from man's best friend.

He should be happy that she didn't mind being seen with him in such a public setting. Instead, he regretted that he might not have a chance to tell her the truth about what he'd really been up to while she was away at college. He'd planned to have that conversation with her today and really shouldn't put it off any longer, not if they were going to have a chance at a future together. And more than anything, he wanted there to be a future for them.

He put the truck in park and said. "Here we are."

She hopped out before he could walk around to help her.

"You know, you never told me you had a dog. He's adorable."

She scratched his bloodhound behind his long, droopy ears. Cole envied him. He handed Josie their red plaid blanket, then grabbed the picnic basket and headed for the back of the truck. "Looks real good ridin' in the back of my truck, don't he?"

"You make a handsome couple."

"Very funny." He lowered the tailgate and took the dog's leash. "Come on, boy."

The dog ambled over to him, but didn't make a move to get out on his own. As usual.

"Lazy hound." Cole set the basket down and lifted the dog to the ground.

"You know, you really shouldn't speak to him that way. He can sense your negativity." To Rick she said, "He didn't mean it, sweetie." Then, he got another scratch behind the ears.

Cole shut the tailgate. "You gotta be kiddin' me."

"No. I read a book about it once."

"Why doesn't that surprise me?" He hefted the basket, and they walked toward the line of people filing into the entrance.

She pushed against his arm and knocked him off the sidewalk. She was surprisingly strong. He found that incredibly sexy.

"He's so gorgeous," she said, returning her attention to the dog. "You're a pretty boy. Yes, you are," she said in that voice usually reserved for small children.

"You'll have him spoiled rotten if you keep that up."

"That's what pets are for."

"Oh, no ma'am. This here's a farm dog. A vicious animal trained to protect me and my property."

Josie began laughing before he even finished speaking.

"What?" he asked, widening his eyes in feigned innocence.

She covered Rick's ears. "This is not an attack dog. I bet he lays around and sleeps all day."

"Yeah, well, we're workin' on that. He just needs a little exercise."

"If you say so."

"Is it okay if we eat before we go into the Fort?"

"That's fine."

"Would you like to set up down by the lake, or do you want to find a picnic table in the shade?"

"That breeze is chilly. I think it would be cold in the shade, don't you?"

"Lake it is, then."

They walked down to the lakeshore arm in arm. Rick loped along beside them. Several families were enjoying lunches and soaking up the sun. Cole and Josie spread their blanket in an isolated spot away from the swings and sand box. They sat, and Rick wedged himself between them.

"Come on. You're killin' me, boy." Cole grabbed Rick's collar and tried to coax him onto the grass.

"Oh, he's fine, Cole. Let him stay."

Josie smoothed her hand down Rick's back and cooed. The dog plopped his head in her lap and stared up at her like he was in love. Cole knew the feeling.

"That's disgusting."

"He's precious."

"Give me a break. He's playin' you."

Josie dug in her huge tote bag, pulling out sunglasses, and a wide-brimmed straw hat. "Jealous?"

"Maybe," he groused.

She smiled and touched his face. "No need. I'm your girl, remember?"

He ran his finger down the chain she wore. The class ring wasn't visible beneath her shirt. "I don't know. You're hidin' my ring."

"I'm a little too old to be wearing someone's class ring on a chain around my neck. And besides," she covered it with her hand, "I like to keep it close to my heart."

"Since that's the way you feel," he reached in his pocket and pulled out a box with a bow on it. "I thought you might like to have this."

She smiled. "What's this?"

"Open it and see."

That smile stayed on her lips while she untied the bow and opened the box. "Oh, Cole!" She pulled out a long gold chain and held it between them.

"I thought this one might be better. The one you have is surely turnin' your neck green. This chain's a little bit shorter. I hope that's okay."

She pulled the other chain out from under her shirt, removed the class ring, made the switch, and put it back on by just putting it over her head. He helped her move her braid out of the way. She touched the ring where it nestled between her breasts.

"It's perfect," she declared.

He'd have to agree.

She leaned over and kissed his cheek. "Thank you."

He stole a real kiss before she could get away. "You're welcome."

She touched the ring again. "How in the world did you find time to get it?"

"I called up Candi over at Heart's Desire. You know, the new salon and, *um,* gift shop?"

"You mean the new place across from the bank? The one that has a sign up that says, 'Naughty and Nice' to go along with the lingerie in the window?"

"Yeah. That's the place."

"I went by there yesterday."

Cole nodded, admiring her shorts and top. She must have gotten them from the Nice boutique, but on her, they looked more than nice. "I called Candi and she hooked me up. Turns out she sells jewelry, too. I met up with her before church this morning."

"Is that why you were late?" Josie put the hat on and slid dark glasses onto her nose.

"Late? The choir hadn't come in yet."

"They're always late, and you're avoiding the question."

"It was one of the reasons." He wasn't ready to get into the other reasons why he'd been running behind, so he steered the conversation in another direction. "What's with the hat?"

"I burn easily." She fished in the large bag

for a tube of sunscreen and began rubbing it onto her arms and legs. His throat closed way before she began smoothing the white cream into her silky thighs.

"Need some help?" he offered, his voice husky.

She gave him what could only be defined as a smoky look. "Probably not a good idea."

*"Mmm."* He found he couldn't look away as she made long, sweeping strokes down her calf.

"Cole!"

He reluctantly raised his gaze to meet hers. "What? I can't even look?"

She chewed her lower lip. "I guess I'm just not used to being looked at that way."

He found that hard to believe when he'd been having exactly these kinds of fantasies about her practically every moment since he'd seen her sitting on that park bench right after she got back into town. "Come on. I know you had boyfriends in college."

Josie shook her head. "Too busy studying." She wiped her hands on a napkin then handed him a sandwich from the basket.

"Surely you didn't study twenty-four/seven."

"Pretty much."

"Man. What about dates?"

"A few in graduate school. All very proper,

usually formal outings. You know, dinner, a museum, the opera. Nothing like this."

He unwrapped his sandwich and took a bite. "Sounds exciting," he lied. Did she consider this a step down?

"What about you?"

Cole shrugged.

"No girlfriends, fiancées, wives?"

"I dated a few people. Nothing serious."

"Why not?"

She offered him a bottle of cold water. He uncapped it and took a long drink. Could he say that in the back of his mind, he'd been waiting for her to come home? Naw. That'd freak her out for sure. "Just waitin' on the right girl, I guess."

She fingered the chain around her neck, but didn't comment. Instead, she shifted her focus to his dog. "Rick looks hungry. Did you bring anything for him to eat?"

"He had a huge dish of food before we left this morning. He only gets to eat twice a day. As lazy as he is, if he ate more, he'd be too fat to walk."

Josie and the dog both gave him pitiful looks.

"Can he have a bite of my sandwich? Please?"

Under any other circumstances, he wouldn't be able to refuse her anything, but he said, "Not a good idea."

"Just one bite?"

Let's see. How could he put this delicately? There was no way. He'd just say it and hope she wasn't offended. "Table food gives him gas."

Josie giggled.

"You won't think it's funny when he lets one rip."

She laughed harder. She looked happy, relaxed, and incredibly sexy. Did he dare believe she was finally his? He kept waiting for the other shoe to drop. For her to suddenly realize this was a huge mistake just before she ran hard in the opposite direction.

Rick, as if sensing the meaning of their conversation, looked crest-fallen. Josie scratched his ears. "Oh, I'm sorry, sweetie."

"You know, he can't understand what we're saying," Cole pointed out. "He's a dog."

"But he's sensitive, aren't you? Yes." She stroked his ears with both hands as she spoke. The dog loved every ounce of attention she showered on him.

His dog had horned in on about enough of his date. He pulled a tennis ball out of a pocket in his cargo shorts and said, "Here, boy. Go get it." He tossed the ball. It rolled to the edge of the lake.

Rick looked at him as if to say, *You must be joking.*

"Go get it, Rick," he repeated.

The dog just swung his head back to Josie and thumped his tail.

She laughed. Not just a giggle, but a grab the stomach, tears rolling down the face laugh.

"You're not helping."

"Oh — oh, I'm sorry."

But she barely got the words out before she lost it again. Cole stood to go retrieve the ball. To the dog, he said, "Next time you come along with me on a date, you're bringin' your own girl."

Josie's laughter followed him as he went after the ball. When he stood next to it, he turned to look back at Rick and Josie sitting all snug on the blanket. "Here, boy." He slapped his thigh and pointed to the ball. "Come and get it."

The dog just thumped his tail.

"Stupid mutt."

"Cole!" Josie held her hands over Rick's ears. "He can hear you," she said in a loud whisper.

"Good grief."

Cole grabbed the ball and walked back up the slight incline to the blanket. He dropped the dog's toy next to Rick, then sat and ate his sandwich. As he chewed, he figured now was as good a time as any for him and Josie to have the talk he'd been avoiding. He needed to be totally upfront with her. About everything.

Taking a drink from his bottle of water, he watched her. She nibbled at her sandwich and petted Rick. She seemed so happy. How would she react to what he had to say? No sense pondering the matter. He should just jump in, get it over, and deal with the fallout. Maybe he'd get lucky and she wouldn't be too upset.

"Josie?"

*"Mmm?"* she chewed her sandwich, swallowed, and chased it down with a drink of water.

"There's something I need to tell you." He wadded up the waxed paper she'd wrapped his sandwich in and tossed it into the basket.

"Sounds serious."

He had her full attention. Cole cleared his throat. "I guess it depends on how you look at it." Right now, he found he couldn't look at her. "After dad got sick, there was just me and my mom, and she was getting older and wasn't able to take care of the farm without Dad's help. So, I had to drop out of school to take over running the farm."

Josie nodded.

"At nights, I continued to study. Several of the teachers from the high school tutored me so that I could get my GED."

"That's wonderful, Cole."

"Well, what you don't know is that —"

Rick chose that moment to nose the ball against Cole's hand. His bark sounded more like a soulful bellow from a bugle.

"In a minute, boy."

Josie picked up the ball and threw it. Rick loped off after it, but instead of bringing the ball back, he got distracted by the remains of a picnic lying on a vacated blanket.

"Rick, get away from there," Cole called after the hound. The dog just ignored him.

"You'd better go get him," Josie said.

"Sorry. I'll be right back. Rick!" He chased down the dog and grabbed his collar to pull his head out of a bag of chips. "Bad boy."

Rick looked properly contrite, casting him woeful puppy dog eyes.

"Come on, man. You haven't acted like this since you were a pup. You interrupted an important conversation."

Rick just hung his head as they walked toward Josie. Before they made it back, a short, thin man approached her. A black miniature poodle wearing silly pink ribbons accompanied him.

Cole heard the guy say, "Josephine, is that you under there?"

The man bent to peer at Josie under the wide brim of her hat. She put her hand on the cap and looked up at him.

"Martin. Hello."

"Fancy meeting you here, darling."

Cole bristled. This guy had no right to call his girl "darling." Rick ran ahead and resumed his position beside Josie. He obviously thought she could protect him from further scolding.

"I'd no idea you had a dog. He's rather, *um,* large." The tiny poodle standing at the end of a thin, red leash beside him eyed Rick cautiously.

"Oh, this isn't — I mean, this is Rick."

"Charming name for a bloodhound. How do you do, Rick? May I present Fifi?"

Introducing dogs to each other? Cole rolled his eyes heavenward. Fifi. What a ridiculous name for a dog. Must be a disease of people who were supposed to be refined and sophisticated. Rick sniffed the poodle and wagged his tail. The poodle pranced. No accounting for taste.

When Cole reached the blanket, he just stood there, waiting for Josie to introduce him to the little man. He'd seen the guy around town, but couldn't say they'd ever met. Josie shifted her gaze from him to the other man, a look of sheer panic on her face. He decided to help her out.

"Cole Craig," he held his hand out to the smaller man. Instead of shaking it, he looked at Cole's hand then up at his face.

"Craig? As in a Craig of the back of the ridge Craigs?"

Cole shoved his hand into his pocket. *Here we go,* he thought. "The same."

To Josie he said, "Do you *know* this man?"

"Yes, we went to school together. Cole, this is Martin McKay."

Ah, the new bank president and Harvard boy. Rich Daddy's heir apparent who'd gone to exclusive private schools instead of the public institutions he and Josie had attended. "McKay." Cole nodded to the little man who appeared to be stunned.

"Do you mean to say," he wagged his bony finger between them, "the two of you are here? To-geth-er?"

Rick growled at Martin. Cole smiled. He'd get a treat for that later.

Josie patted the dog's head, and he settled down. "We were just having sandwiches."

Was it him or was Josie trying to downplay the fact that they were out together?

"In-deed?"

"Yeah. You never had a sandwich, Marty?" Cole abbreviated the name just to annoy him. He'd say it worked, judging from the red splotches staining the man's cheeks. "I think we have a few more in the basket. Josie does *amazing* things with peanut butter, if you know what I mean." He wiggled his brows and smiled.

Josie still wore that expression of panic, and his last statement seemed to have ratcheted that up a notch. Cole felt contrite. The last thing she needed was him starting something with Old Witch McKay's son, especially after the encounter he'd had with the woman this morning at church. The little weasel was sure to beat a path to his mommy's door with this tidbit of gossip. Not that he cared, but she *was* Josie's boss. Still, Cole couldn't seem to help himself.

Martin continued to ignore Cole.

"Cole helped me out with a burst pipe a couple of days ago."

There she went . . . downplaying again. He tried not to feel the sting of hurt at her words.

"Really?"

It was like some demon drove him. "Yeah. And I caulked your windows last week, Marty."

"I am sure I would not know as our housekeeper deals with such matters."

"In-deed?" Cole mimicked.

Josie bit her lip to keep from laughing.

"Well, I never!"

"He's just kidding around, Martin. He wasn't trying to insult you."

"In-deed," Cole confirmed.

A smile tugged at his mouth. He caught Josie's eye. Her mouth quivered, her eyes danced. When she shifted her attention back to Martin, a light of recognition flashed in his dull, brown eyes. It would be clear to anyone — even Martin — that something was going on between him and Josie.

"Tell me, Josephine, did you work last evening as you said you must?"

Josie looked uncomfortable again.

"I don't think that's any of your business, Marty," Cole supplied.

"Martin!"

The weasel actually stomped his foot!

Rick began growling again. Josie soothed the dog. Cole just smiled, making Martin even more angry.

"That — *um* — *dog* of yours looks like it's anxious to get out of here," Cole said.

The poodle was pulling at its leash, clearly worried that Rick had directed his growls at her.

"You're as uncouth as your — your — mutt!"

Rick growled again.

"Careful. That 'mutt' has a purer pedigree than you, McKay."

"Well, I never!"

Cole smacked Martin between the shoulders. "Well, you know what that say. There's a first time for everything."

"Josephine, I am shocked that you would deign to consort with an individual who possesses such a singular lack of breeding."

Cole just kept smiling. "If all people with breeding act like you, I'll take that as a compliment."

"You would."

The situation transformed from worse to nightmare status when Rick chose that moment to "break wind." Martin looked at Cole, obviously thinking him the culprit.

"Rick, buddy," Cole scolded the dog.

"How rude!"

That's when Josie lost it. Utterly lost it. She laughed so hard, no sound came. She doubled over, holding her hat to keep it from falling off. Rick sniffed her face and licked at the tears streaming down her cheeks. When Cole joined in the merriment, Martin turned on his heel and marched off, his dog in tow.

Cole fell onto the blanket holding his side and his nose. Rick looked particularly pleased with himself. He had, after all, gotten rid of Martin.

When the laughter subsided, Cole touched Josie's hand and said, "Are you okay?"

"I think I may have bruised a rib."

"Well, it's your own fault. I told you Rick here couldn't tolerate table food, and still, you sneaked him some, didn't you?"

"He was hungry," she said, still smiling.

He nodded in the direction of the rapidly departing Martin. "That little weasel always so obnoxious?"

Josie could hardly say "yes" through the laughter that bubbled up again.

Cole got serious. "Is he gonna cause trouble for you?"

"He'll try, but don't worry. I can handle Mrs. McKay."

"Are you sure?"

She leaned over and kissed him . . . a soft gentle caress that seemed to buoy her confidence. "Yeah."

"I know how much you love your job. Our relationship won't jeopardize your position, will it?"

"You didn't finish lunch. I have fruit salad."

She dug in the basket and pulled out a

square, plastic container.

"Josie —"

She removed the lid. "It has grapes, strawberries, melon, cherries, and this wonderful cream cheese sauce —"

"Forget the fruit."

She picked out a fat, juicy strawberry and slowly licked some cream off it. *"Umm . . ."*

Cole's gaze locked on her tongue and then her mouth as it closed around the tip of the ripe, red berry.

"So, before Martin and Rick interrupted us, you were about to tell me something," she was saying.

"You're changing the subject and trying to distract me with fruit."

She held the strawberry she'd just bitten to his lips. He couldn't resist.

"Is it working?"

"Maybe." He bit into it. "I keep losing my train of thought."

"You're avoiding my questions, as well."

He grasped her hand and made a methodical process of licking the sticky, sweet sauce from her fingers.

"I'm sorry about Martin. I shouldn't have goaded him," Cole said.

"No, you shouldn't have."

He continued to lick her fingers. "What will he tell Mrs. McKay?"

"I really don't care."

"I don't believe that."

Josie smiled and leaned over to kiss him. "I'm not surprised, because yesterday, even this morning, I couldn't have said that. But, it's true. I really don't care what he tells his mother. Don't worry." She leaned forward. "It'll be fine," she said against his lips.

Cole pulled away, but kept her close. "I won't stand for you losin' your job because of me, Josie Lee."

"I won't lose my job. I'm too valuable."

If only he had her confidence. Knowing Old Lady McKay, she was sure to have a cow when she found out about him and Josie. And that could mean nothing but trouble.

He hadn't bargained for this. He'd been so bent on pursuing her, he hadn't considered the price she'd have to pay for being with him. She needed his protection. He didn't know how he'd manage it, but he'd do whatever it took to make sure she wasn't humiliated in front of all of Angel Ridge by the McKays.

# CHAPTER 10

They finished their lunch and spent the rest of the day exploring the encampment. It was a beautiful day, tailor made for just this sort of event. Fort Loudoun was one of the most beautiful places in the area. Pre-Revolutionary, it had been a British Fort placed in this location to deal with the Cherokee Indian settlement that had been nearby. That worked pretty well until the Cherokees decided they'd had enough of these foreigners in their midst and took control of the Fort. After that, the British pretty much just high-tailed it back over the mountains to Charleston.

All that remained were some buildings that had been replicated by the historians who ran the museum. The most spectacular thing about the Fort was its view — it sat on the banks of what had been the Little Tennessee River, and the mountains of North Carolina rose up behind it in spectacular fashion.

Josie looked out across the expanse of Lake Tellassee that had been formed by the dam the Flood Control Board had built some fifty or more years earlier, flooding the valley and its homes, forcing the residents up onto the ridge. Beautiful.

Cole remained unusually quiet. He didn't even give her tidbits of information about the architecture of the buildings like she'd expected. He always loved talking about the old buildings around town. Instead, he quietly bought them rock candy made by the ladies dressed in colonial dresses. Later, they'd held their ears when, on the hour, the uniformed British Regulars fired the cannons. Josie's ears still felt a little numb from all the noise.

Not another person recognized her as they mingled with the crowds of people filling the Fort. Not even Minnie Reed, and she'd been her mother's best friend for as long as Josie could remember. At this point, however, Josie really didn't care who saw her on Cole's arm. After their encounter with Martin, something had changed. She realized that she had feelings for Cole. Deep feelings. And she didn't care who knew it. She removed the straw hat and carried it as they walked from building to building.

"Aren't you afraid you'll burn?" Cole asked.

"Not any more."

She'd spent too many years weighed down by the expectations of this town. She was tired of trying to be someone she wasn't, if she even knew what that was. She'd like the time to explore just that notion. She refused to let the expectations of narrow-minded people affect her personal life or what she wanted for the future. That included dating the man of her choice. And she chose Cole.

He was everything a woman could want and more. Tall, handsome, dependable, trustworthy, an upstanding member of the community, fun to be around, intelligent, sexy, a great kisser. . . .

"What's that look all about?" Cole asked and they stopped to examine a display of quilts.

She had looped her arms around his as they strolled through the displays. She must have been staring up at him with a lovesick look on her face and hadn't realized it. Ignoring his comment, she asked a question of her own. "I was just wondering why you've gone all quiet. You've been acting funny since that run-in with Martin."

He shrugged. "It's like I said. I don't want him causing trouble for you."

"Why don't you let me worry about the McKays?"

He squeezed her hand where it rested against his arm. "I don't want you to have to worry about anything."

"I can handle it." She wasn't sure how she'd handle it, but she was determined that she would. She hoped her smile showed more confidence than she felt.

"Has Mrs. McKay already said something to you?"

She didn't want to tell him the woman had warned her off him only a couple of days ago, so she just said, "Not really. Can we buy some more rock candy? I've finished mine already, and it was so good. I haven't had it in years."

"Sure." He pulled out some bills and handed them to a woman wearing a traditional, Revolutionary Era dress.

Josie selected a bag of the candy while Cole chose a sucker that had the candy clustered around its end. He popped it in his mouth. She began salivating. Not for the candy in her bag, but for the taste of it on his tongue.

Pulling him away from the crowd of people, she asked, "Want to share?"

He slowly removed the treat from his mouth and held it out to her. Josie grasped his wrist and slid her tongue from the bottom to the top of the candy attached to the stick. She purposely caught his fingers in the process.

He sucked in a ragged breath. "Keep that up and we'll be out of here in record time," he warned.

She trailed a finger down his chest. "We could be back at my house in about five minutes," she suggested, in a low, husky voice.

Cole grabbed her hand and headed for the exit. Rick barked as Cole jerked his leash. "Sorry, boy."

Josie had to jog to keep up. Her laughter trailed behind them, causing more than a few heads to turn.

The sun was just setting behind the mountains rising up behind the lake, when Cole unlocked the door to his truck and helped Josie inside. After he'd settled Rick in the back and gotten in, he started the engine and said as Josie slid over close to him on the bench seat, "I hate to bring this up, but you said you needed to go in to work."

She removed her glasses, then snuggled up against his arm and nibbled his neck. "It can wait an hour or so."

Gravel flew as Cole threw the truck into gear and roared out of the parking lot. "You sure you don't want to go back to my place? It might be more private."

"Too far."

He got them there in record time. Josie hadn't stopped kissing and touching him all the way back to her house. He followed the drive around to the rear of the house to where a garage had been added on. When they hurried for the back door, Rick whined his displeasure at being left behind.

"Stay, boy," Cole said.

Josie looked back at the hound. "He can come in."

The dog would probably jump right in the middle of them if he did. Cole wanted no distractions. "He'll be fine." Thankfully, the hound yawned and lay back down.

The door clicked shut behind them after they entered her kitchen. Cole wrapped an arm around Josie's waist. "Come here." He smoothed a hand down her back and pressed his lips to hers. She tasted like fresh air, sunshine, strawberries, and true love. He wanted nothing more than to melt so far into her that neither of them would know where she began and he ended.

Josie broke the kiss, but he couldn't stop tasting her face, her neck, the curve of her shoulder. When her shirt got in the way, he slid it off her shoulders and eased it down her arms until it lay in a puddle on the floor at her feet. Underneath, she wore a pale pink snug fitting shirt with thin little straps that he wanted to watch slide down her arms leaving all that creamy skin bare for him to explore.

The gold chain he'd given her sparkled against her skin. The class ring was hidden between her breasts beneath the fabric. He trailed the backs of his fingers across the exposed skin above the shirt's low neckline. She shuddered and grabbed handfuls of his shirt.

"Cole . . ." she breathed.

"Tell me what you want," he encouraged.

She leaned into him so that he couldn't read her eyes. "Give me a second," she said against his neck. After a brief pause that seemed like an eternity to his overcharged hormones, she continued. "Could we go into the sitting room?"

He nodded, and she led him into a small room off the back hallway that had a couch with deep cushions, a chair and a fireplace. She stopped at the couch and sat. Cole followed.

Josie crossed her legs and faced him. She took his hands in hers and laced their fingers. She acted like she was working through something in her mind. He wanted to take her in his arms and finish what they'd started in the kitchen, but he just waited for her to make a move. Give him an indication of where her head was.

After a few moments had passed, she said, "Cole?"

He couldn't stand it any longer. He reached around behind her head and laid her braid across her shoulder. He removed the band securing it and began to run his fingers through the braid to loosen it. *"Hmm?"*

"Remember yesterday when I told you I didn't know how this worked, and you told me that nothing would happen that I didn't want to?"

He almost groaned. Had he been stupid enough to say that? Sheez. He'd meant it at the time, but now with her sitting so close, knowing they were all alone in her house with a bedroom somewhere nearby. . . .

"Yeah."

"Would you believe me if I said you're the first man I've really enjoyed kissing?" She closed her eyes and leaned forward to lay her head on his shoulder. "Oh, and I feel so much when you kiss me."

Even though he was surprised, her pronouncement made him insanely happy. He wanted to be the first and last man she'd ever kiss. He tipped her chin up. "Then why are we talking when we could be —"

He captured her lips and plunged his tongue into her mouth. God, he wanted so much. He wanted to show her how much he needed her, show her everything he felt for her, make her his forever. He pressed her back against the pillows, loving the way her hair spilled out behind her.

"Cole?" she said before he could kiss her again.

*"Hmm?"* he said as he trailed a hand down her thigh to her knee.

"I missed a lot growing up. I never had time for the things other girls did, because there was school, and I was always studying."

"It's all right. I promise to catch you up on everything you missed out on."

She smiled. "Really?"

He nodded. "Tell me what you want to do."

She wrapped her arms around his neck, and he couldn't resist further exploring hers with kisses.

"Well . . . I missed the prom. Don't guess we can make up for that."

"There's the Snow Ball in December, right before Christmas. I'd love to take you to that."

Her smile was pure happiness. "Okay."

"What else?" he asked, as he traced the line of her jaw with his fingertip. God, the thought of being with her at Christmas made him insanely happy. December was more than six months away. This confirmed she was thinking of them being together that far down the road. He wasn't just a fling for her.

"I want to date someone. Have a boyfriend and all that entails."

"I'm all yours. What does having a boyfriend entail?"

"Going to movies and stealing kisses." For good measure, she leaned up and touched her lips to his, then continued. "Going parking up in the tall pines."

"Well, we've done the tall pines, but we can go again and neck in the truck if you want. How 'bout tomorrow? We could catch a movie, too."

"*Mmm,* tomorrow's going to be really busy for me. How about Tuesday?"

"It's a date." He brushed the hair back from her face and asked, "Anything else?"

"I just want this feeling to last. Want to see if it will grow. Want to take things slow. Don't want to miss a second of anything that's happening between us."

Cole smiled. "God, you're so sexy when

you talk in the present tense."

Josie's pure laughter danced around them in the quiet house. He wrapped his arms around her waist and held her tight. "What do you want to do right now, Josie Lee Allen?"

She ran a hand up his neck, and then smoothed it down his hair. As long as he lived, he'd never tire of the feel of her hands on him.

"You'll think it's silly. I'm sure you've done it a dozen or more times with other girls."

He leaned back and looked into her eyes. "There's no one but you. There won't be anyone but you." There had been others, but he'd never wanted anyone like he wanted her.

"I know," she said softly.

"So tell me what you want. I'll give you anything, just tell me."

She chewed on her lower lip. "I want to neck."

"What?"

"I don't know exactly how, but I'd like to try it . . . with you."

He laughed. "Well, it's pretty much what we've been doing. Lots of kissing, heavy breathing, touching." He trailed a hand back down her smooth thigh. "If we were still teenagers, there might be a hickey involved."

She eased a hand under the hem of his shirt and slid it up his side before exploring his back. "I've never had a hickey. Is it hard to do?"

He focused his attention on her neck. He loved the scent of her perfume that clung there. Loved the way she tipped her head back when he kissed her there so he'd have better access. "No, it's not hard, but you might have trouble explaining it at work tomorrow."

"I could wear a scarf."

He skidded a thumb across her throat. "They usually last for several days, and it's not exactly turtleneck weather."

*"Mmm."* She touched his neck. "What if I gave you one?"

"That might be hard since you don't know how it's done."

Her smile was slow and sexy. "I didn't say I don't know how. I understand the mechanics. I just haven't ever had one, or given one."

"Don't tell me. You read about it in a book."

"I've read romance novels."

"So, are you saying you'd like to give me one?"

"Maybe. After we've necked for awhile."

Dear Lord. And she wanted to take things slow. Bypass the cold shower. He'd just pick up a ten-pound bag of ice at the Quik Stop on his way home and sit with it in his lap for the rest of the night.

Still, he said, "Happy to oblige."

"You won't mind if people see it?"

He shook his head. "You'll have a hard time keeping me away from a mirror. Every time I look at it, I'll think of you and how you gave it to me."

"So what are we waiting for?"

Josie loved the way Cole was looking at her almost as much as she loved the thought of him being hers. Hers and no one else's. In education, she'd excelled, always gotten A's, but in relationships, especially with men, she'd flunked miserably, never even trying. She knew her limitations. She was short with red hair and pale skin. No great beauty. But when Cole looked at her the way he was now, she felt like the most beautiful woman in the world.

They kissed again. Josie explored the expanse of smooth skin beneath his shirt, all she could reach anyway. He was still seated and leaning over her, touching the exposed skin of her legs and arms. She wished she could touch more of him.

She broke the kiss, slid her lips across his face to his ear and asked, "Do you mind if we switch?"

He swirled his tongue along the outer edge of her ear, pushing her to the limit of sanity. "What do you mean?"

"Can I be on top?"

That got his attention. He sat back and looked at her, clearly surprised.

Josie took advantage of the latter. She pressed him back against the opposite arm of the couch and crawled between his legs. "Now I've got you where I want you."

"Honey, you've had me where you want me longer than you can imagine."

"Too bad I didn't know. I might have taken advantage of you sooner."

He circled her waist with his hands, hitching her further up against his chest. "Is that what you're planning? To take advantage of me?"

"Maybe." She teased a finger down the V created by the opening in his unbuttoned polo shirt. "I bet you're not used to women taking advantage of you."

"I could get used to it with you."

She scraped her teeth across the nearly unperceivable cleft in his chin. The afternoon stubble lining his jaw felt rough against her face. Chill bumps erupted across her body. "Where would you like your hickey?"

"*Mmm*. Surprise me."

"Let's see . . ." She slid her hands down his throat and opened his collar further, then used her tongue to trace a line from his ear to the place where his neck blended into his shoulder. She nibbled there. "*Mmm* . . . that's a nice spot."

The scent of his cologne clung to all the right places, teasing her nose as she dipped her tongue into the concave V at the base of his throat. A kiss began there that ended at the curve of his neck just below his chin. She stopped to nibble a bit there as well. "That's a nice spot, too."

Cole was getting restless beneath her. She smoothed a hand across his chest. "Patience," she whispered as she began an exploration of the other side of his neck.

"I guess now would be as good a time as any to tell you that patience has never been one of my strengths."

"Then you know that the only way to gain patience is to have it tested."

"Anyone ever told you that you'd make a master tormentor?"

She stopped nibbling the spot behind his ear and looked into eyes that had turned navy blue. "I'm sorry. I don't mean to torment you."

"Don't stop."

"Are you sure?"

He slid his hands up under her shirt in back, pulling it up in the process. "Don't ever stop."

Josie returned to the place where his neck ended and his shoulder began. "I think I'll put it here. It'll be our secret spot. No one will know it's there but us." She nibbled and sucked until the spot became red. "Does it hurt?"

"So good . . ." he moaned.

"Do you think that was enough to do it?"

"Might want to work on it a little more, just to be sure."

She obliged. As she kept working, he ran his hands over her back, her arms, her legs . . . After several moments had passed, she kissed the spot, then looked at him. "Your turn." She tipped her head to the side, inviting.

Cole sat upright, supporting her back with one hand and guiding her legs around his hips. She sucked in a breath as if she were surprised. Now he had her attention.

He slowly eased her hair back over her shoulder, then hooked a finger under the thin strap of that pretty pink top that had been tempting him for the past half hour or so. "I think this might be in my way."

"Of giving me a hickey?" she asked.

"Yeah."

She smiled. "But it's not anywhere near my neck."

"Who says hickeys have to be on your neck?"

Her eyes widened. "Oh. Where do you think . . . oh . . ."

He eased the strap down her arm and explored every inch of her shoulder and collarbone with hot, open-mouth kisses. Her skin tasted as good as her kisses. When he was satisfied he'd enjoyed every inch of that shoulder, he worked his way up her neck to her cheek. "I wonder if the other side tastes as good?"

She shrugged the shoulder in question. "Maybe you should find out."

Cole stared deeply into her eyes as he wrapped the other strap around his finger. "This will have to go."

She wet her lips with the tip of her tongue and grabbed two hands full of his shirt, pulling him forward. "Of course."

He captured that tempting tongue while he pulled the other strap down over her shoulder. He didn't know how that blasted pink top stayed in place, but true to his word, he explored the other shoulder, kissing his way from her lips to her neck, across her shoulder, and back across her collarbone. Josie tipped her head back, exposing her neck to him completely. Her long hair teased the forearm he had pressed to her back. The shirt slipped lower as she arched her back, exposing the creamy upper curves of her breasts.

Cole groaned. More than anything, he wanted to ease that top down to her waist and see her wearing nothing but his class ring and that chain. But he also didn't want to frighten her by moving too fast. She'd said she wanted to neck. She hadn't invited anything further. But he was nothing if not human. He was beyond tempted.

"Cole . . ."

He buried his face in her hair and struggled for control. His chest rose and fell rapidly from the effort, making matters worse. His chest brushed her breasts with every breath.

The phone rang shrilly, offering them both a reprieve. When she didn't move to answer it on the third ring, Cole said, "Shouldn't you get that?"

She sank her hands in his hair and said, "The machine will pick up in a second. Kiss me again."

"But —"

The machine picked up as she blew him away with a mind-altering kiss. For a woman who claimed to not have much experience kissing, she sure was a quick learner. She'd just deepened the kiss in amazing fashion when the machine's jarring "beep" sounded, and Mrs. McKay's voice filled the entire downstairs.

"Josephine Allen, pick up the phone this instant. This is Harriet McKay. Hello?"

Josie jolted back. A hundred emotions raced across her face and through her eyes. She eased away from him and off the couch. While she was in the kitchen getting the phone, Cole collapsed against the couch cushions, trying to recover.

When she came back into the room, she didn't rejoin him on the couch. She looked upset, pacing in front of the fireplace. Agitated. She raked a hand through her hair, then crossed her arms. "That was Mrs. McKay."

He had gotten that, but he said, "What did she want?"

"It's those reports I was going in to work on. She wants them now." Josie shifted her weight and pushed her hair back again. "I should, I mean, I need to —"

"Go." he supplied.

"I'm sorry. It's just that those reports

234

aren't anywhere near finished. If I start now, I might be able to get them to her by," she checked her watch and groaned. "I didn't realize it was so late."

Cole stood and stepped in front of her. He rubbed her arms. "Want me to give you a ride?"

She rested her hands against his chest. "I'd rather stay here with you, but I guess that's not an option."

"We'll have plenty more nights to neck."

Josie smiled. "Do I have a hickey?"

He pushed her hair back over her shoulders and checked the skin exposed above her top. She'd replaced the straps. He ran a finger along one. Josie shivered at his touch. "I had a little trouble deciding on a spot. Maybe next time."

She moved in closer. "Promise?"

He enfolded her in his arms. "I promise."

She tugged at his collar. "Let me see yours?"

"How's it look?"

She grabbed his hands and urged him into the hallway. "See for yourself."

They stopped in front of a mirror that hung over a hall table. Cole moved his collar aside. There it was.

"How did I do?"

He wrapped an arm around her waist and

drew her in for a quick kiss. "It's perfect, just like you."

She seemed immensely pleased with his compliment. Confident and sure of herself.

"Let me drive you into town." He wasn't ready to leave her.

"Thanks, but I could be there awhile. I think I'll take my car."

"You're sure?"

"Yeah. I'll walk you out."

They held hands as they retraced their steps to his truck. Rick lifted his head and whined as they approached. She stroked one of his long ears. "Oh, it's okay. We'll see each other again real soon. I promise."

The dog wagged his tail.

"Maybe your daddy will take me to your house next time."

"Maybe," Cole agreed.

When he opened the door to his truck, Josie reached behind the seat for the picnic basket and her bag. Cole blocked her access by taking her hands in his. "How 'bout if I bring the basket to you tomorrow?" he suggested. "That way, you won't have to deal with it now."

She turned to face him. "Fill it up, and I'll meet you in Town Square for lunch."

"Well, I'd have to check my schedule . . ."

She gave him a playful smack on the arm.

Cole laced his fingers with hers. "*Um, Josie?*"

"*Hmm?*"

"Mrs. McKay, did she say anything to upset you?"

A breeze blew his hair across his face. She reached up to push it back. "Don't fret about Mrs. McKay."

"I can't help it."

"I'm a big girl. I can handle Mrs. McKay."

"Nah, you're just a little thing."

Josie laughed again. "Thanks for this weekend." She touched the class ring. "For everything."

"Don't thank me yet," he warned.

"Would you quit worrying about Mrs. McKay?"

He raked a hand through his hair and looked away. "You sure you don't want me to drive you over to the library? I could come back and pick you up when you're finished." And maybe if he stuck around, he could help run interference with Mrs. McKay.

"There's no need for you to go to all that trouble. I'll just drive myself."

"I don't mind."

She touched his face and said, "Kiss me and tell me you'll see me tomorrow."

He leaned down and kissed her, slow and

sweet and thorough. "I'll see you tomorrow." He rubbed his thumb back and forth across her kiss-swollen lips.

She pressed a kiss into his palm. "Tomorrow."

He just stood there for a moment and watched her walk away. Before she entered the house, she turned and took a step back toward him.

"I almost forgot. Earlier, at the Fort, you said you wanted to tell me something. We never got around to that."

Cole's blood ran cold. He'd forgotten, too. Convenient. "No worries. We'll talk about it tomorrow."

"You're sure?"

He just nodded. He hated like crazy watching her walk away again without telling her, but it was not a conversation he wanted to have when he didn't have all the time he'd need to deal with her reaction.

Rick barked his goodbye. Josie waved before disappearing from view. Cole reluctantly got into his truck.

Mrs. McKay was going to cause trouble for her. He knew it as well as he knew his own name. He couldn't let that happen. He'd have to figure out a way to make sure that meddling old woman left Josie alone.

# CHAPTER 11

Josie hurried to the room she used as her home office, gathered her papers, and stuffed them into her briefcase. Mrs. McKay would be waiting for her at the library. Josie could just imagine it. The woman would probably be standing by the front door, tapping her foot impatiently, wondering why Josie hadn't magically appeared there immediately after their phone conversation had ended.

Josie smiled. Maybe she'd enjoy the nice weather and walk. She tossed her keys in the air, locked the back door, and walked between her house and Miss Estelee's, heading for the sidewalk that would take her into town.

"Howdy-do there," Miss Estelee called from her front porch.

Josie waved at her neighbor. "Oh, hello Miss Estelee. I didn't see you sitting there." This would make her even later getting to the library. Good.

"I 'spect you haven't seen much besides that young man in the better part of a week."

Josie smiled and diplomatically evaded the topic of *that young man.* "Nice day we had. I hope you were able to get out and enjoy it."

"You're a gettin' in way over your head, Missy. Some folks up here won't take to the likes of you consortin' with the likes of him. You'll see. But you just gotta trust that them angels knows what they're a doin'. Don't dance to them fancy folks's tune. It's high time some of you young people danced to your own tune. *Mmm-hmm.*" She nodded and rocked back in her chair.

"I'll keep that in mind, Miss Estelee. If you'll excuse me, I need to go in to work for a bit. Good evening."

"Oh, it's gonna be a dandy one. You just hold your ground."

Josie couldn't help shaking her head at the senile old woman as she strolled on toward the sidewalk.

"Yes sirree, it's gonna be a sight to behold."

Miss Estelee laughed, and the sound of her humming floated on the warm spring breeze that followed Josie down the street.

When she arrived at the library, she noticed that Mrs. McKay stood at the front door, impatiently tapping her toe against the brick porch. Just as she'd suspected.

"Good evening, Mrs. McKay," she called out a greeting as she approached.

"Well, here you are. And what exactly is the meaning of this, young lady?"

"I beg your pardon, ma'am?"

"Why are you not in your office? Why did I have to call you at home?"

"It's Sunday evening, Mrs. McKay. The library isn't open on Sunday evenings."

"Yes, but I am certain your work is not completed on Friday at five."

"Which is why I'm here now."

"Indeed? I am surprised that you have the time. I am also aware that you did not report to work yesterday."

"I'm off on Saturdays, Mrs. McKay. It's in my contract."

"Evenin', ladies," Constable Harris walked by and tipped his hat.

"Good evening, Constable Harris," Josie said. Mrs. McKay didn't reply. A sidewalk on Main Street was not the place to have this discussion.

"Mrs. McKay, would you like to come in?" Josie unlocked the front door of the library and held it open for the older lady.

"Yes, as a matter of fact, I would."

Mrs. McKay marched past her. Good thing Josie hadn't decided to climb in the window like Cole. She'd been really tempted to, effectively avoiding the old biddy all together. In the end, she had figured Mrs. McKay would have had a stroke if she'd witnessed it. That stroke might evidence itself anyway. Her benefactor was clearly upset.

As soon as they entered Josie's office, Mrs. McKay said, "Josephine, it has come to my attention that you have been seen in the company of a certain young man of late."

"I'm seen in the company of many people, Mrs. McKay."

"I am speaking of the Craig boy."

"Yes, he's been helping out at my house," she evaded. Even though she'd expected it, she still couldn't believe this. Surely the woman didn't actually think she could dictate with whom she spent her time.

"Indeed? And are lunches in the Town Square part of his assistance at your home? Not to mention afternoons carousing together before the entire town."

"Mrs. McKay, I —"

The woman held up a bony, wrinkled hand to stop Josie's words mid-sentence. "I tried to give you the opportunity to make good decisions on your own. However, since you seem incapable of doing so, I will say this once, Josephine, and know that I invite no discussion on the matter.

"I and the other members of the McKay Foundation Board deem it wholly inappropriate for you to be consorting with *that* young man."

Josie blinked. Miss Estelee had said the exact same thing not fifteen minutes ago.

"Mind you, he has his purposes here in town. He is a hard worker and does his family name proud, but he is not cut from our cloth," the woman said succinctly. "You would do well to seek out the company of someone more your equal in social status and education."

"Someone like your son?" Josie supplied.

"Precisely. You and Martin would make a splendid couple."

"Mrs. McKay —"

"I do not believe it necessary to remind you that the McKay Foundation funded your education and pays your salary here at our library. We expect our town librarian to conduct herself in a respectful manner."

A warm breeze stirred the curtains at her window.

"I was not aware that I had conducted myself in an inappropriate manner, ma'am."

243

"Of course, if you are in disagreement with me, your contract with the Foundation could be easily terminated. However, we would expect reimbursement of the fees paid for your graduate studies. I'm sure you understand."

"Yes, I understand." She understood that this bigoted old woman thought she had just skillfully nailed her to the wall. Josie's family didn't have that kind of money lying around in the bank, and they'd never think of selling the house, so the woman would naturally think there was no way she could come up with the funds to pay the Foundation back for the best graduate education money could buy. She had no recourse legally against a private foundation.

There was something, however. Josie smiled. Clearly Mrs. McKay had not thought this through.

"Good. I'm glad we had this little chat, dear. I'll tell Martin you're in need of an escort. Good evening."

Mrs. McKay stood, turned on her heel, and marched out of Josie's office. Josie followed the domineering woman as far as Teresa's unattended desk. "Mrs. McKay?"

She stopped. "Yes?"

"I am sorry to inform you that your conditions are not at all acceptable to me. I fear I shall have to resign my position with the library."

"What?" Mrs. McKay seemed genuinely stunned. In fact, she was quite unattractive with her mouth agape.

"It's really too bad. The trials I've been putting my cataloging system through show the program is ready to be implemented and interfaced with the library's new website."

Mrs. McKay stood facing Josie, rigid with indignation. "The program will remain whether you stay or go, you ungrateful chit."

"No, I'm afraid not. You see, the program is mine and is copyrighted in my name. I have had numerous lucrative offers for the software rights, but money was never an issue for me. Loyalty to the Foundation and my hometown are of greater importance. Or were. I will remain for two weeks while you search for my replacement. Good evening." Josie walked back into her office.

"Wait just a minute, young lady. The Foundation owns that program. We paid for your education."

Josie closed her window, then sat in her desk chair and faced Mrs. McKay, her fingers steepled before her. "Yes, but I created the program, and you do not own my mind, or me for that matter."

"Josephine, don't be so hasty. Let's discuss

this a bit further."

"I can't see that there is anything to discuss."

"The Foundation should at least be afforded the opportunity to purchase the program from you."

"It is not in my best interest to sell the program at this time, Mrs. McKay. I prefer to secure a library directorship where I would be free to work unencumbered and allowed to implement the system. I do not have to tell you that there is no other cataloging system such as this in the nation. It won't be difficult to find a prestigious institution willing to allow me to write my own terms of appointment."

Mrs. McKay sat heavily in the chair on the other side of Josie's desk. "And what would those terms be if you stayed here?"

"In return for exclusive use of the cataloging system for two years, I would hold the position of director of the library with a ten percent increase in pay, a seat on the Foundation board, my educational debt canceled . . . and never mentioned again," Josie said succinctly.

"Five years," she countered.

"Three."

"Deal." Mrs. McKay stood. "I'll have the

Foundation's attorney draw up the contract."

"Fine," Josie agreed. "Oh, and I assume I need not mention that my private life is my own. It is of no one's concern."

Mrs. McKay hesitated in the doorway of Josie's office, but at last glanced over her shoulder and said, "Of course."

Josie nodded and leaned back in her chair as Mrs. McKay disappeared from view. She'd done it. She slapped her desk with the flat of her hands. At last, she was totally free. She stood and spun around, stopping to face the window.

Cole. She pushed the window open and sat on the sill. She leaned out a bit, hoping against hope that he would be there. He wasn't.

She relaxed against the window casing and took a deep, cleansing breath. Her first without the stifling expectations of this town and her indebtedness to the Foundation weighing on her.

She and Cole . . . They'd be free to have an open relationship. She'd like nothing better than to go now and find him to tell him her news. Her gaze fell on the unopened briefcase sitting on her desk. Those reports still had to be finished.

Tomorrow. She'd tell Cole everything at

lunch tomorrow. He'd said he would meet her in town for lunch. She hoped she could convince him to take her up to the tall pines for a much more private celebration.

A secret smile stayed glued to her face as she completed the work on the reports. Everything was finally falling into place. The job of her dreams, a wonderful man who was crazy about her, and a life in the town that she loved. Maybe Miss Estelee was right. Those angels were working their magic.

Cole fumed all the way home. How dare that old woman threaten Josie's job because of her relationship with him. He slammed his fist against the dash.

He shouldn't be surprised. He'd known that this was exactly what would happen. It's why he'd followed Josie back to her office. He'd stood outside the window and heard all the hurtful things that woman had said to Josie. It had been all he could do to not intervene then and there. But that would have only made matters worse, so he'd forced himself to leave when they'd entered the outer office.

No. He'd bide his time. Come up with a plan. He'd show them all who he was. Who he really was. He'd become a man Josie could be proud to be seen with in front of the haughtiest of Angel Ridge society. He and Josie would thumb their noses at them all. He'd see to that.

# CHAPTER 12

The next day, Josie anticipated Cole appearing at her window all morning. When noon came and went, she walked down to the Town Square. Cole hadn't called to further discuss their lunch plans this morning. Maybe he just expected her to meet him at the angel monument.

She hoped she'd either find him sitting on the bench near the monument, or maybe walking down the sidewalk toward the library, but the park bench stood empty. She scanned the streets, expecting his disreputable looking truck to be parked somewhere along Main Street, but she didn't see it. Thinking that he might be running late, she sat and waited. When the courthouse clock tolled two, she returned to the library.

She spent the rest of the day with half her mind on her work, the other half tuned to any sign of Cole. She didn't even have the board meeting to distract her because Mrs. McKay had postponed it a day. With all the reports completed the night before, all she could think about was Cole. Where could he be?

As the sun began to set, Josie kept glancing from her computer screen to her window, but he never came. On her walk home, Josie encountered Constable Harris.

"Evenin', Dr. Allen." He tipped his hat.

"Good evening, Constable."

"You wouldn't happen to have seen the Craig boy today, would you?" the man asked.

Surprised that he would ask the very question that had been on her mind, she responded, "No, I'm sorry." She waited, hoping he'd offer more information. He didn't disappoint.

"Strange. Cole didn't show up for any of his appointments in town today. It's unusual for him to say he'll be somewhere and then not come."

Josie agreed. That wasn't at all like Cole. She wondered if he might be ill.

"Well, I won't keep you. Good evening."

Josie nodded and continued down the street toward her home. The more she thought of Cole's absence in town today, the more concerned she became. When she walked up her sidewalk and saw that Miss Estelee's grass hadn't been cut, she grew even more troubled. Cole never failed to mow that lawn on Mondays.

"It's a terrible shame," Miss Estelee was saying. She shook her head and rocked in time with the movement.

"Oh, it isn't too awfully bad, Miss Estelee. I'm sure Cole will be by tomorrow to cut it." They'd had a cooling shower overnight. It was probably still too wet today for mowing.

"A shame, I say, the way some folks treat other folks like they got no soul."

"I beg your pardon?" Josie said, confused.

Miss Estelee rocked forward, pointing a crooked finger at Josie. "You can't judge a book by its cover. That's what I always say. And you ought to know that better'n anybody, Missy. *Mmm-hmm.*" She leaned back and rocked harder, her old chair squeaking its protest.

Josie's frown deepened. She didn't have the presence of mind to try and sort through the old woman's verbal maze. Not tonight. She was too worried about Cole.

Inside, she went straight to the kitchen and pulled out the phone book. Craig. Craig. She trailed her finger down the list of Craigs to the *C*'s. No Cole listed. She flipped the book shut and began pacing the kitchen. Absently, she pulled the class ring from beneath her blouse and moved it back and forth against the chain.

Why hadn't he come to town today? Why? Could he be having second thoughts about them? Something had been bothering him when he left her house yesterday. He'd been worried about Mrs. McKay. He'd also needed to talk to her about something. Maybe that was it. They hadn't had a chance to get into it, but he'd promised they would today.

She couldn't believe he had stood her up. They'd made plans. He'd promised that he would see her today. Promised. And he'd stood her up.

Josie propped both hands against the island and leaned forward, her eyes closed. No. Cole would not intentionally stand her up. There had to be an explanation.

She straightened and faced the window over her kitchen sink. Maybe he just had things to do at his farm. He'd been spending a lot of time in town with her. It was spring after all. There must be hundreds of things to do on a farm. Still, why hadn't he called?

He'd probably show up tomorrow as usual for lunch with a plausible explanation. After all, they'd only been seeing each other for less than a week. He didn't have to check in with her. She turned the class ring in her hand. She had no real claim on him.

The next day, Josie hardly made it through the morning. She was so anxious to see Cole that she had to force herself not to run to the Town Square at noon. When she reached the angel monument, she again found him missing.

She sat heavily on the wood and wrought iron seat next to it. Where could he be? She looked around town, at the faces of those milling about. The one face she ached to see was curiously absent.

*Think, Josie, think. Who might have seen Cole?* Maybe Mr. DeFoe had seen him.

She hurried down the block to the hardware store that's exterior had seen few changes in the last hundred years. Its long brick façade took up most of the block. A new, dark green awning with the name of the business in white letters extended over the sidewalk. A bell tinkled as she entered the cool interior.

"Howdy-do, Miss Josie," Mr. DeFoe called out a cheerful greeting.

"Hello, Mr. DeFoe."

"Beautiful day to be alive and livin' on

the ridge, ain't it?"

Was it a beautiful day? She hadn't noticed. The sunshine seemed to have disappeared with Cole. "Mr. DeFoe, I was wondering if you could tell me whether or not you've seen Cole Craig?"

"Sure I've seen him. Everybody sees Cole. But I can't say as I seen him this week."

Josie blinked. "I'm sorry. Did you say you *had* seen him?"

"Sure," the ancient old man nodded.

"Have you seen him this week?"

"No, can't say as I have."

"Is that unusual, Mr. DeFoe?"

"Well, now that you mention it . . . let's see, this is Tuesday. *Uh-huh.* And Cole, he normally comes in on Monday or Tuesday to get his supplies for the week. That'd been yesterday or today."

"Right," she agreed, thinking to help him along. "Did Cole come in yesterday or to-day?"

"Nope. I ain't seen him. Why?" He leaned across the counter, his eyes narrowed. "Was he supposed to do something up at your place?"

"No, it's just —"

"Now mind you, it ain't unusual for Cole to disappear for weeks at a time, but it is unusual for him to say he's gonna do somethin' and then not do it. You see, he was supposed to fix the front door on the church. We can't git the dang thing to lock. And the preacher said Cole told him on Sunday he'd take a look at it, but he ain't showed up to fix it yet. And I did see the preacher yesterday. He's in a right fine state what with not bein' able to lock the church and all. So, if Cole turns up at your place —"

"I'll mention it to Cole if I see him. Thank you, Mr. DeFoe." Josie retraced her steps to the door, but before leaving, turned and said, "Mr. DeFoe? How do you usually contact Cole when you need him? Do you call him?" Maybe he could give her Cole's phone number.

"Nope. Like I said, I always see him around town. No need to ever call."

"Well, thanks again, Mr. DeFoe." Josie stood motionless on the sidewalk outside the hardware store.

Where could he be? She again scanned the streets of the town, hoping to see him strolling along. A host of familiar faces greeted her, but none that made her heart race. Ferguson's was right across the street. Maybe he'd been by there.

Josie crossed the street, walked in the open door of the diner, and went straight to the counter. There was barely room for her to elbow her way through the lunch crowd filling the place almost to capacity.

"Well, look what we have here. Our newly-crowned town librarian comin' in for lunch. Will wonders never cease? She finally stopped working to eat. Shove over, Fred." Dixie smacked the library's maintenance man with her order pad. "Give that seat up to this hungry woman."

Josie touched Fred's shoulder as he started to rise. "That's not necessary, Fred. I'm not here for lunch," she said to Dixie.

"What?" Dixie consulted the oversized, fuchsia dial of her watch. "It is lunchtime, and I feel sure you haven't eaten. From the looks of it, you've not had much sleep, either. Still burnin' the midnight oil over at the library?" She leaned in closer and continued so only Josie could hear. "Or is that fine lookin' Cole Craig keepin' you up to all hours?"

She wished. "That's why I came by. I was hoping that Cole might be here." She scanned the crowded confines of the diner, praying she'd catch a glimpse of him.

"He's not here, hon. Come to think of it, I haven't seen him since church on Sunday."

"Is that typical?" Josie asked.

Dixie shook her head. Her spiked, mahogany tresses didn't budge. "Not if he's in town. He's by here for breakfast and lunch most days."

"If he's in town. What do you mean by that?"

"You know, if he has things scheduled to do for people. Otherwise, he don't come into town."

Josie propped her elbows on the counter and rested her head in her hands. She'd grown up in Angel Ridge. Why hadn't she noticed before now that no one here spoke in comprehensible sentences?

Dixie came around the counter, took Josie's arm and walked her into a back office. "There now, that's better. I could barely hear myself think out there. You want to have a seat?"

"No. I should get back to the library. Dixie, I know this seems a strange question to ask, but do you know how to get in touch with Cole?"

"No. I don't think I've never had to call him. If I need him, I just catch him when he comes in to eat."

Josie nodded. That seemed to be a recurring theme, troubling her even more. Why hadn't he been into town?

"Thanks, Dixie. Sorry to have troubled you. I know you're busy."

"No trouble. Let me give you a sandwich to take back to the office."

"Thanks, but —"

Dixie held up a hand, halting her words. "Never let it be said anybody left Ferguson's hungry."

She opened the cooler and pulled out a bag containing what Josie guessed was a chicken salad sandwich. She'd bet her last dollar on it.

"Thanks, Dixie." Josie reached for her purse and realized she didn't have it. She raked a hand through her hair. She'd never been this out of sorts in her life. She didn't like the feeling.

"I'll put it on your tab," Dixie offered.

"Thanks. Dixie?"

"Yeah?"

"Do you know where Cole lives?"

"Well sure. He doesn't live too far from my folks's farm."

"Can you tell me how to get there?"

"Well, I could, but I don't know that I should."

"Dixie, I really need to see him. I'm afraid something's happened to him."

Dixie hurried over to the doorway and called out, "Blake? Come here a second, would you?

"Now listen here, Josie. Like I said, it ain't

unusual for Cole to stay out at his place, sometimes for days, even weeks at a time."

"But we were supposed to meet yesterday for lunch," Josie said. "He didn't show up and he didn't call."

"Well now, that is strange. That's not like Cole at all."

"Yeah, Dixie?"

Blake Ferguson joined them. He was what most would describe as tall, dark and handsome in a James Bond kind of way. But he didn't appeal to Josie at all. She preferred tall, golden, and sexy as sin.

"Seems Cole Craig has gone missing and Josie wants directions out to his place."

Blake shook his dark head. "You don't need to be goin' out that way by yourself, Miss Josie."

Blake shifted his weight and put his hands in the pockets of his jeans. He avoided making eye contact with her. Josie thought he looked uncomfortable. Was she imagining that?

"Why not?"

"Because, you have to drive through Shady Hollow."

"So?"

"Well, you know Old Man Crane's place is out there, and he shoots at strange cars."

"You're kidding."

"Oh no, ma'am. It ain't safe. Now he wouldn't bother me. I've done some work on his house. Put in a central heat and air system for him a few years back."

"Maybe you could take her out there," Dixie suggested.

Hope bloomed in Josie's heart.

Blake looked at his watch instead of her. "Well, I wouldn't mind to, but I've got an appointment up in Maryville at one."

Josie's hopes shattered. "That's okay."

He touched her arm. "My guess is you'll see him soon enough."

Josie wished she had his confidence. To Dixie, she said, "If you see Cole, would you ask him to come find me at the library?"

"Sure, but I agree with Blake. If he shows up in town, I'm guessin' you'll see him before anyone else."

Josie elbowed her way through the diner and stepped out into the bright afternoon sunshine. She couldn't shake the feeling that something was terribly wrong.

She hurried back to the library, hoping against hope she'd run into Cole on the way. With no sign of him, she entered the quiet library. The smell of books usually soothed her, but not today.

She bypassed the hallway to her office and went directly to the reference section. Stopping in front of one of the shelves, she pulled down the city directory and carried it to her office. Maybe Cole's phone number would be listed in this.

Teresa stood and said, "Josie, there's a messenger waiting for you in your office. He has a delivery."

Impatient, Josie asked, "Why didn't you sign for it?"

"He said he had specific instructions that only you were to sign for it."

"Oh, for heaven's sake." Josie entered into her office. She didn't have time for this.

A uniformed courier stood and said, "Dr. Josephine Allen?"

"Yes, yes," she took his clipboard and said, "Where do I sign?"

"Line two."

She signed her name and handed the clipboard back to the man. He took it, gave her a tube along with a flat, business-size envelope, then left.

Josie tossed both on her desk unopened and thumbed to the *C*'s in the city directory.

"What is it?" Teresa asked.

"Teresa, can't you see that I'm busy!" Josie's voice was a bit sharper than necessary, and she immediately regretted her loss of control. "I'm sorry. I'm a little on edge."

"Ya think?" Teresa's smile softened her reply. "What are you looking for?"

"A phone number."

"Did you order a map or something?" her secretary asked, studying the cylindrical tube on Josie's desk.

A map. That's exactly what she needed. Maybe there was a way to circumvent Shady Hollow. When she looked up, her secretary was still hovering. Josie gave her what she hoped was a warning look.

"Sorry. Mind if I open it? I'm dying of curiosity."

"Please," Josie said, then silently added, *just leave me alone.*

Craig. Josie dragged her index finger down the list of Craigs until she stopped on Colen. Colen MacAllister Craig. Two twenty-three Craig Hollow Road. No phone number listed. "I need a road map," she said.

"It's a blue print." Teresa rolled the contents of the tube out on the surface of the small, round conference table in Josie's office. "I didn't know the library was building a new wing."

"We're not. We can hardly afford to execute Phase One of the cataloging program. That's why I've been trying to write a grant for computers all week while you scan data for the special collections."

"This has a computer room," Teresa said. "And look at all the computers!"

Josie frowned and walked over to where Teresa *ooh*ed and *ahh*ed over the drawings. There were two color computer models. One, an outside view of the wing, the other of the inside. She was looking at all the computer equipment she needed to fully implement her system. This was what she'd envisioned, knowing that it would take years before the McKays would let go of enough cash to do anything of this magnitude.

"Oh my gosh! I don't think I've ever seen a check with this many zeros!" Teresa exclaimed. She'd opened the flat envelope and now extended a check to Josie.

It was a cashier's check made out to the Angel Ridge Library for an obscene amount of money. More than enough to build and equip the dream that lay before Josie. "Is there a letter?" Josie asked.

"No. Nothing. Just these drawings and the check," Teresa replied.

She must have made more of an impression on Mrs. McKay than she realized the other night. She couldn't believe the board had done this. Josie returned to her desk, picked up the phone, and hit her speed dial for Mrs. McKay.

"McKay residence," the maid answered.

"Hello, this is Dr. Josephine Allen. May I please speak with Mrs. McKay?"

"Certainly. One moment."

"Yes, hello?" Mrs. McKay's clipped voice snapped through the line.

"This is Josephine Allen."

"Yes, yes. What is it?"

Josie bristled at the woman's tone. Ever cordial. "Blueprints just arrived for a new wing to the library along with a cashier's check which I assume is funding for the project. I wasn't aware the Board had approved funds for a new wing. I'm thrilled, of course —"

"I beg your pardon? Have you gone daft, young lady? The Board has approved no such thing, and as I am sure you are aware, funds for such a venture are not in our immediate future. As I've stated, you will have to make do with the computers you have."

"But I have architectural plans and a check."

"You must be mistaken. Perhaps this delivery was made to the library in error."

"Mrs. McKay, I can assure you there is no mistake." Josie further explained the drawings and the amount of the check made out to the library.

"Well, I've never." Mrs. McKay sounded

outraged. "The funding for the Angel Ridge Library has been fully endowed by the McKay family for more than a hundred years. Who in the world would make such a donation without first consulting my family?"

"I am sure I have no idea, ma'am."

"Well, we shall have an immediate meeting of the board thirty minutes hence in the conference room of the library. Have your secretary make the necessary arrangements." The line went dead.

"Great," Josie mumbled, and hung the phone up. She'd have to postpone her trip to Cole's.

She gave Teresa her instructions and found a road map while her secretary organized the emergency board meeting.

The meeting began precisely thirty minutes after Josie's call with Mrs. McKay had ended. Josie should be excited. The realization of her dream for the library she would run lay in the middle of the long mahogany conference table, but she found she couldn't concentrate.

While the board members debated . . . Who could have made such a donation? Who would presume to have plans drawn up without asking for the board's input? All

Josie could do was wonder what had happened to Cole? Where could he be? Had he lost interest? Had he, in the end, considered her just another snob from the ridge?

"Dr. Allen, please inform this young man that we are in the midst of an important meeting," Mrs. McKay was saying.

"I'm sorry?" Josie turned then and saw Cole walking confidently into the conference room, as if he belonged there. "Cole!" Josie rose halfway out of her seat, intent on launching herself into his arms, but caught herself just in time. He looked so different. He'd cut his hair into a shorter, more conservative style and he wore gray dress pants, a crisply starched white shirt open at the neck, a navy blazer, and dark, casual dress shoes. He seemed somehow . . . different as well. More refined. His bearing more confident.

"Dr. Allen," Cole nodded in her direction. "Ladies and gentlemen of the Board, I see you received the plans for the new wing. On behalf of CMC Designs and the Craig family, let me say how pleased I am to be working with the library on this project."

"What?" someone interjected.

"On behalf of the *Craigs?*" another said in a sarcastic whisper followed by a chuckle.

Mrs. McKay gained her composure first.

"Do you mean to say that you're throwing your hat into the ring first for the contractor's position, Mr. Craig? Well, I'm not sure how you heard about it so soon," she shot Josie a look, then continued. "May I just say that this project is a bit . . . sophisticated for your simple skills? Of course, I'm sure there will be a need for skilled laborers such as yourself," she finished smugly.

"Actually, Mrs. McKay," Cole removed a business card from a pocket inside his jacket and offered it to the woman, "I took the liberty of speaking with Blake Ferguson. He's a fine contractor who lives here in Angel Ridge. I feel his firm is well-suited for this project. He assures me he can begin the grading of the south lawn as soon as next week. Or, if you prefer, we could break ground as part of the town's Memorial Day celebration."

A stunned silence settled over the room. Mrs. McKay looked at the card in her hand and then leaned forward to ask, "What is the meaning of this, Mr. Craig?" She held the business card toward him. "Do you actually expect us to believe that you are an architect employed by the firm of CMC Designs? How utterly absurd! CMC Designs, though a relatively new firm, is renowned throughout the southeast as one of the most innovative in the industry."

"Thank you, Mrs. McKay. That's high praise coming from you."

"You're an architect?" Josie blurted out. "But —"

"Yes, do tell, Mr. Craig. How does a high school dropout become an architect?" Mrs. McKay practically snorted.

"Harriet," Mr. McKay held up a hand to his wife, "let the man speak."

A look of outrage passed across Mrs. McKay's face, but she settled back into her seat.

"No. That's a fair question, and one I'm happy to answer. After my father's illness forced me to leave school, I earned my GED. Since I was able to work at my own pace, I got my diploma earlier than I could have if I'd stayed in school.

"Then, I took some of the money my family made from selling off a parcel of the Craig property for the shopping center at the edge of town and enrolled at the University of Tennessee. I was accepted to the school of architecture in my second year, and by doubling up on courses, was able to complete my studies in four years.

"With the help of a computer, I began my own firm. I bid jobs via the Internet, came to be on a first name basis with the overnight deliveryman, and got my start.

"My vision for CMC is to create architectural designs for towns such as Angel Ridge that complement and blend in so that the historical integrity of the community is not compromised."

"What does the CMC stand for?" someone asked.

"Colen MacAllister Craig," Josie quietly supplied. She had totally bought his act. She'd fallen for Cole Craig, the simple handyman who was always willing to help out. Cole Craig, of the back side of the ridge Craigs, who'd always been looked down on by those who lived up on the ridge. Cole Craig for whom she'd risked her job. Cole Craig who had stolen her heart. Cole Craig who had duped them all.

There was poetic justice in it, really. Sitting here watching a Craig put all these snooty people in their places. Herself included. But the question begged to be asked, "Why? Why have you done this?"

Cole looked into her eyes, his feelings for her exposed for all to see. "I'm interested in seeing the new automated cataloging system and website you've developed in use, but in order for the system to be completely operational, the library will need a fully equipped computer wing."

"This is quite a grand gesture, Mr. Craig," Mrs. McKay said. "One I am sure you are aware the board will be unable to refuse. For we, too, are anxious to see our Dr. Allen's innovative system running at full speed. Although I feel certain your motivation in this is somewhat obvious, the library and community will nevertheless benefit from your generosity."

Cole nodded to Mrs. McKay. It was the closest he would come to getting an invitation into the inner circle.

"The board will adjourn for now, but will reconvene this evening for our scheduled meeting at seven, if that would be convenient for you, Mr. Craig? I'm sure we'd all like to go over these plans in more detail."

"Of course," Cole replied.

As the meeting adjourned, Josie stood and retreated to her office. How dare he? How dare he manipulate and humiliate her this way!

"I do not wish to be disturbed, for any reason, Teresa," Josie said just before she slammed her office door with a satisfying crack. She removed her blazer and flung it across the room.

"You're upset?" Cole asked, disbelief lacing his words.

Josie spun and faced the man she'd been

frantically searching for all week. She hadn't heard him enter her office. "Who do you think you are?"

Cole closed the door more quietly than she had. He took a step toward her. She held her ground, ready for this confrontation.

"I thought you'd be pleased."

"Did you? Tell me, Cole, after all these years of deception, why wait until now, this moment, to reveal yourself?"

"You want the truth?"

"Yes, that would be a refreshing change."

"Sunday night, when you were in your office with Mrs. McKay, I was standing outside your window. I overheard what she said to you about your associating with someone like me. I didn't know what else to do, Josie. I didn't want to lose you, but at the same time, I didn't want you to lose what you'd worked your whole life for."

"So you thought you'd ride in on your white horse and save the day?"

He took another step forward, his hands held out in front of him. "What kind of man would I be if I had the means to help the woman I love, and I didn't use it?" he asked gently.

Her heart constricted at his declaration of love, but warred with her resolve to be free of this sort of manipulation. First Mrs. McKay and now Cole. Though she longed for his love, she refused to allow him to do to her what this town had done to her all her life. Obligate her.

"If you'd stuck around and eavesdropped a bit longer the other night, you'd have heard me resign my position here. Then you would have had the pleasure of hearing me tell Mrs. McKay that if I went, the cataloging program would go with me. By the time I walked out of here, I had a raise as director, a seat on the board, and a canceled debt for the graduate education the McKays financed. And now, here you are, trying to buy my job security and buy yourself a place on the social register as a bonus."

"I don't care anything about that, or at least I didn't before my being a simple handyman was someone who wasn't good enough for you to date."

"That didn't stop me."

"You can't deny that you were embarrassed to be seen with me."

"It wasn't that. Certain things had to be dealt with."

"And I've dealt with them."

Josie advanced until she stood nose to nose with Cole. "No, I had already dealt with them. Something you would have known, if you'd bothered to talk to me about it. I kept telling you I could handle Mrs. McKay, but I guess you just didn't have any faith in me."

"Josie —"

"Let me tell you something, Colen MacAllister Craig, I can achieve job security all on my own. The McKay Foundation is lucky to have me and don't think the board doesn't realize it." She shook her head. "After all the years you had to put up with those snobs slinging their money around and looking down their noses at you . . . You're no better than they are."

She snatched up her purse and headed for the door.

"Josie, wait."

He grabbed her arm to halt her progress.

There was no way she could overpower him, so Josie just stared at his hand and quietly said, "Let go of me, Cole."

"Josie, please. Can't we talk about this?"

She looked up into his brilliant blue eyes and somehow found the courage to speak the words that would put an end to their relationship. "I have nothing more to say to you."

Cole's hand fell away. Despite the fact that she could feel her heart shattering within her chest, Josie walked out of her office, her head held high, without looking back.

# CHAPTER 13

The next week passed with agonizing slowness even though Cole kept busy with preparations for the new library wing's groundbreaking that would be part of the town's Memorial Day celebrations. There were a million things to finalize. Plans to fine-tune, consultations and meetings with Blake Ferguson, suppliers delivering materials.

The meetings with Josie had been the worst. They'd had to discuss the placement of the computers and how many would be needed, system requirements and infrastructure. All the while, he'd only wanted to be alone with her. To take her in his arms and kiss her until nothing else mattered but the feelings they had for each other.

Did she even miss him? Had she ever really cared about him or had she just been slumming with a Craig from the wrong side of the ridge? Maybe she'd already gone back to the rich professor types she was used to.

Without thinking, he pounded the table with both fists, rattling the silverware and sloshing hot coffee over the rim of his cup.

"Easy there, Hercules." Dixie wiped up the amber liquid just before it spread over the edge of the table and hit the floor.

"Sorry, Dix," Cole mumbled.

"Shove over," she said as she slid into the booth next to him.

He did as she said. "I'm not the greatest company," he warned.

"Yeah. I got that. It's clear to anyone with eyes that you're not sleepin', you're not eatin' — or if you have been, you've not been doin' it in here. You've thrown yourself into that project over at the library, but you been walkin' around town like some kinda big bear with a thorn in its paw. Well, I've got good news. I'm just the woman to yank it out."

"I wish it could be that simple."

"It looks pretty simple from where I sit."

He shook his head. "You have no idea."

"I know more than you think. In fact I know too much, and I can't believe the half of it."

He slumped down in the booth. "Come on, Dix. You know how diner gossip can blow things out of proportion."

"Then set me straight. Tell me that it's not true. Tell me that the Cole Craig I have known since I was a kid did not masquerade about town as a handyman when all along he was some big shot architect who just happens to be filthy rich."

Cole winced. Leave it to Dixie to boil the facts down and throw the filth that floated to the top in his face. "Is it as bad as you make it sound?"

"If spendin' the past ten or so years livin' a lie is bad, then answer your own question."

"If you call lettin' people believe and see want they want livin' a lie, then I guess I'm guilty of that."

"Oh, no you don't." She pointed a finger at him. "Don't you put this off on the 'snobs living on the ridge.' You were happy enough to become one of them when it suited you."

"I did that for Josie. If it had been up to me, I would have left things like they were."

"Oh, yeah. That would have been much simpler. Keep to yourself and never let anyone close enough to know the real Cole Craig. Which is it today? Are you here as Cole, the good ole boy handyman, or as Colen MacAllister Craig, CEO of CMC Designs?"

"They're the same person. I'm no different today than I was a week ago, a month, a year."

"And if you believe that lie, you're worse off than I thought. Falling in love changes things. In fact, it changes everything. And once it happens, there's no goin' back. So the question is, now that you're out of the closet and your business has been exposed to everybody in town, what are you going to do?"

"I don't know what you mean."

"Well, you can't go back to the way things were. Folks around here will treat you different now. They already are."

She was right about that. Not one person had asked him to do anything this week. He'd even gone by the church and tried to fix the busted lock on the sanctuary door, but Pastor Strong had refused his help. Said he planned on fixing it himself. Even Miss Estelee'd had a boy from the high school cut her grass.

Cole shrugged. "Maybe it's time for me to move on. The business has grown beyond what I can handle on my own. I need to hire a staff. I've got several jobs going in Georgia, and I've bid some more. Maybe I'll move down there and open up offices in Atlanta."

Dixie set back in the booth and pinned

him with a look. "Oh, now there's a plan. Run away from this mess you've created instead of stayin' here and dealing with it like an adult."

"Why do I get the feeling that the subject just shifted to Josie?"

"As far as I'm concerned, that's the only subject that needs discussing. Folks up here can think what they want of you. People, like me and Blake, who care about you, will forgive you and the rest can — well, the rest just don't matter. Now, Josie, I would think that she matters."

"She doesn't want to see me."

"Well of course she doesn't."

Cole looked at Dixie surprised. "Have you talked to her? Did she say somethin' to you?"

"She doesn't need to say a word for anybody who's lookin' to see that she's heartbroken, same as you."

Hearing what he already knew put into words made him feel even more miserable. "Everything I did was for her."

"No. Everything you did was for you. Men . . ." Dixie sighed. "I don't guess we can blame you for being male. When will you ever learn?"

"Speak English, Dixie. I'm lost."

"Is it not the twenty-first century? Do we,

the capable, competent women of today, have anything about us that indicates we need a man to rescue us? No!" she said, answering her own question. "Take Josie. She may be small, but that is just about the most capable woman I have ever seen. She's brilliant, always has been. You know that. She has a Ph.D., for heaven sake, in library science. They don't just hand those papers out to anybody who asks for one. She worked hard for what she has and earned it because she knows her stuff.

"Sure, Mrs. McKay thought Josie would come back here and be her little puppet on a string, but I had no doubt that when the time was right, Josie Lee Allen would put that woman in her place. The problem was that you didn't have that same confidence in her. It was her business. Her battle. And you tried to take that away from her."

Cole's chin dropped to his chest. "I didn't mean to."

She squeezed his hand. "I know that. My guess is that Josie knows it, too." She paused while he digested that bit of information before continuing. "She was angry, and rightfully so. She's a sensible woman. Now that she's had time to cool her jets, I'm sure she sees things differently. You should talk to her, not run off to Atlanta."

"I don't know."

Dixie stood and smoothed her apron. "It's a risk. But if you love her, I'd think it's a risk worth takin'. Now clear out this booth. I got payin' customers waitin' to be seated."

As she walked away, Cole reached into his pocket and pulled out some bills to leave on the table. When he passed Dixie, she was taking an order. He stopped and leaned down to kiss her cheek. "Thanks," he said.

Dixie seemed speechless. That had to be a first.

When Cole walked out of the diner, he wondered if what Dixie had said could be true. He looked down the street toward the library. Should he do what she had suggested and just go talk to Josie?

No. He should do this right. He wouldn't just walk into her office with his hat in his hand. He'd really show her how he felt. It was like Dixie had said. It was a risk, but he loved her. The alternative of not having her in his life didn't bear consideration.

Tomorrow was the town Memorial Day Celebration. If he was going to woo the town librarian back into his life, he'd better get to work.

Josie's heart just wasn't in it. She had seen Cole nearly every day around town for the past week, but he'd kept his distance. That was what she had wanted, after all. She took perverse comfort in the fact that he looked as miserable as she felt.

Now the preparations were at an end. She sat on the front steps of her home, trying to summon the will to take herself into town for the day's events. She didn't know how she could possibly give the appearance of being in a festive mood when she felt so alone and unhappy.

"The course of true love never did run smooth," Miss Estelee commented. Josie's neighbor sat in her customary spot on her front porch, rocking, enjoying the spectacular view of the lake. "I think the Apostle Paul said that."

Josie stood and slowly made her way over to stand in Miss Estelee's front yard. "No, I believe that was Shakespeare, ma'am."

"No, no. That was the Apostle Paul speaking to the Corinthians."

Josie smiled. No use in arguing. "Were you ever in love, Miss Estelee?" She assumed that the woman knew about what had happened between Cole and her. Everyone seemed to.

"Oh, yes." She rocked in an easy slow rhythm. "He was blond and tall like your young man. Very handsome."

That's right. Josie remembered Cole telling her on their first date about Miss Estelee having been in love. The picnic by the angel monument . . . the memory of it caused the ache in her heart to intensify. She swallowed hard. "But you didn't marry?"

"No."

A profound sadness seemed to etch the woman's words as well as every line in her time-weary face. She stopped rocking. Became quiet and very still.

"What happened?"

"We were from different worlds. I thought I could live the rest of my days without him. Then I went and did some silly thing to try and make him jealous, thinking he'd . . ." The old lady's words trailed into silence, then she shook off her faraway thoughts. She resumed her rocking motion, this time faster, like she was troubled by her unhappy memories. "It didn't make no difference, 'cept for I found myself in a world of misery.

"I lost everything. Let me tell you somethin', Missy," she stood and faced Josie. "When you're old and alone, like me, with no children of your own to love and no one to take care of you . . . It's a terrible thing havin' to depend on the charity of others when you got no one else.

"What's worse is the knowin'. The knowin' that I could've had so much more than what I wound up with, and the knowin' that I got nobody to blame for it but myself."

With tears shining in her clear blue eyes, Miss Estelee slowly made her way into her house. Josie's chest tightened. She squeezed her arms and turned away. In that moment, everything focused into harsh clarity. Her pride stood between her and Cole. She'd been angry and hurt in the beginning, but now she just felt empty.

She felt her feet drag as she forced herself to walk into town when all she could think of was curling up on the bed in a darkened room and having a good cry.

Instead, she would smile and go through the motions for the groundbreaking while standing next to Cole. She was afraid that pulling that off would require better acting skills than she possessed.

The Memorial Day celebration was a success. As usual, the entire town turned out. She even saw Miss Estelee sitting on the park bench near the angel monument with Doc Prescott fetching her lemonade from the tables Dixie had set up in the middle of town.

Everyone seemed pleased with the plans

Cole and Mrs. McKay presented for the new addition to the library. Pleased that someone they admired had done so well for himself, regardless of which side of the ridge he called home. Well, almost everyone. Some folks up here would never accept Cole, no matter how much success he achieved. He didn't seem to mind. In fact, he looked almost . . . hopeful?

Josie didn't have time to puzzle about it. Shovels spray-painted gold and decorated with red, white, and blue ribbons were given to her, Cole, Mrs. McKay, and Mayor Houston for the ceremonial moving of the first clumps of dirt. Josie smiled and posed for pictures taken by Joe Easterday, photographer for *The Angel Ridge Herald.* Now, with the parade down Main over and the picnicking complete, a magnificent sunset would be the precursor to fireworks over the lake.

Couples walked hand in hand down to the shore with lawn chairs and kids in tow. Angel Ridge always put on a spectacular fireworks display, followed by music and dancing at the gazebo in the Town Square. This was a time for couples. A time for families. Time for Josie to go home and have that cry.

She turned to begin the long walk down

Main to Ridge Road only to find Cole standing in the middle of the sidewalk, blocking her way. He had that familiar red plaid blanket draped over his arm, and the thumb of his free hand hooked into the back pocket of his black jeans.

Even after all that had happened between them, seeing him still took her breath away. Although she hated the shorter styled haircut he'd adopted in his quest for respectability, she had to admit that he looked incredibly handsome. He was wearing that loose-fitting white shirt she remembered from that night he took her up to the tall pines.

He approached her slowly. Josie couldn't have moved a muscle if she'd wanted to. Her traitorous heart kicked into overdrive as he neared.

"I was hopin' I could talk you into joining me for the fireworks."

Josie's racing heart jumped and lodged somewhere in the region of her throat. In her years of growing up in Angel Ridge, she'd always watched the fireworks with her parents. All the while, she'd dreamed of sitting by the lake with a handsome man, his arms linked around her as they watched the fireworks display that would herald the beginning of summer.

Strolling down the hillside leading to the lake with Cole at her side would more than fulfill every childhood fantasy she'd ever had. She sighed. How she longed to spend this and every evening with Cole. But, so much stood between them.

He took another step forward and softly said, "Can we call a truce, Josie? Just for a few hours?"

She looked up into the soft blue eyes of the only man that she'd ever loved and with tears stinging her eyes said, "Yes."

Cole smiled and took her hand. He led her to a spot away from the crowd. He spread the blanket, and then with a hand at her elbow, helped her sit.

"Thank you," she said.

He joined her on the blanket. "Thank you."

He sat so close she could feel his heat, smell the familiar scent of his cologne. Despite the warmth of the late May evening, she shivered.

"Are you cold?"

"No, I . . . No."

Cole trailed a hand up and down her arm in a slow, sweeping movement that did wild things to her tortured, fractured heart.

"I've missed you so much," he whispered.

Days of being without him, without feeling his touch, made her weak. She swayed toward him. "I've missed you, too," she admitted.

He cupped her cheek in his hand. Josie closed her eyes and just let herself feel again.

"Honey, I never meant to hurt you. As Dixie would say, I went all male. I just saw a situation and thought I could fix it. I was an idiot, and I hope you can forgive me."

She knew he was talking about the donation to the library, but she needed to go deeper than that. "Why did you do it, Cole? Pretend to be a simple handyman when clearly, you're so much more?" The clues had been there all along, but Josie had been so overwhelmed by her feelings for Cole, she'd ignored them.

He shrugged and looked away. "These people up here, they've sort of carved out a place for me, and the fact is that no matter what I do, how much money I make, or how many degrees I earn, I'll still be a Craig from the wrong side of the ridge."

"Why couldn't you tell me?"

"I was going to."

Realization hit her. "The picnic at the Fort."

"Yeah. That day sort of got away from me."

"You should have told me from the beginning."

"I know that now."

"Did you think I wouldn't understand?"

"I guess, at base, I wanted to know it was me you cared for, not who or what I am."

"The only thing that ever mattered to me was who you were in here." She pressed her hand against his heart. Its strong, steady beat against her palm brought some life back into hers.

He covered her hand with his and said, "It mattered at first. Even at the end, you were hiding behind a big hat and sunglasses when we were out together."

Josie pulled her hand away, unable to face the hurt in his eyes. "I'm not proud of that, but it wasn't you. I just hadn't figured out how to deal with Mrs. McKay. She knew I was seeing you and didn't approve."

"Why didn't you tell me?"

Josie shrugged. "I guess I was embarrassed. I hated to admit that I had allowed myself to become so indebted to a person that I unwittingly put them in a position to dictate my social life. If I'm so intelligent, I should have been able to keep myself out of that kind of situation."

"You're too hard on yourself."

"You deserved better."

He took her hand and stared at it. "I know what I did was wrong, but I just wanted to be someone you *could* be proud of."

"You were . . . you are." There. She'd said it. She squeezed his hand and dipped her head so that she could look into his eyes as she said the words in her heart. "I'm proud of what you've made of yourself, but I would have been just as proud if you were the town handyman."

Cole gave her a quick, gentle kiss as the first of the fireworks lit up the night sky to the delight and applause of all assembled. Josie could hear the band tuning up in Town Square as they prepared for the dancing that would follow.

The night seemed full of magic with Cole here. In their time together, he'd opened up possibilities she'd never dared dream of for herself. But sitting here with him, the possibility of her spending the rest of her life making a family with a man that she loved seemed within her grasp.

"Come here," Cole said. He pulled her around to sit in front of him so that she leaned back against the solidity of his chest and rested her head against his shoulder. He pressed a kiss to her temple.

"Can you forgive me?"

"Only if you can forgive me for making

you wonder if I could care about you."

"I'll forgive you, if you do care about me."

She turned in his arms and touched his face with her fingertips. "I care about you, Cole Craig."

His smile lit up the night like no fireworks ever could.

She swung around and leaned back against him.

He rubbed his cheek against her hair. "You have the most beautiful hair. I love it hanging loose like this around your shoulders."

He trailed a gentle hand through it. She closed her eyes and sighed as more fireworks sailed into the sky over the lake.

"You know, I think I've loved you since you were a little girl. While you read those books at recess, I'd try and make sure the ball rolled near you at least once so I could get a look at the title of the books, and after school, I'd go down to the library and check them out."

"Really?" Josie smiled up at him.

Cole grinned and nodded. "I especially liked your Mark Twain phase. And when you were older, the Shakespearian sonnets. I dreamed of reciting them to you, but I never got the chance." He paused. "Things might have been different if . . ."

"If you hadn't had to drop out of school?" Josie supplied.

"Who knows? I mean, you never even noticed me."

"I noticed you," Josie insisted. "How could I not have with the way you used to stand up for me when all the other boys teased me?"

A slow smile brought the brightness back to his eyes. "Remember the time the oldest Jones boy — Jack — flipped your dress up in back." Cole laughed. "You were so embarrassed."

Even now, her face grew warm at the memory. "I was mortified."

"I blacked his eye out behind old man Wallace's barn for that."

Josie felt her jaw drop. "You didn't."

His smile returned, this time mischievous, as he looked down at her. "Those sure were some pretty pink panties, Josie Lee."

"Cole Craig!" She felt her face redden even more.

A big red heart lit up the sky. The words inside it read, *"Cole loves Josie."*

Josie gasped.

Cole whispered against her ear, "I love you, Josephine Lee Allen. Please say you'll forgive me."

"Oh, Cole." She shifted and rested her

hands against his chest. Tears stung her eyes when she said, "There's nothing to forgive." Leaning forward, she pressed her lips to his. "I love you, too," she whispered.

He pulled her closer and kissed her for a long, breathless moment. When at last he released her, he said, "Thank goodness, because this next one would have been real embarrassing if you'd walked off and left me sittin' here all alone."

Josie frowned. Cole pointed up at the sky, and when she looked up, she saw another red heart. The words inside this one read, *"Marry me?"*

She hadn't noticed before, but every eye in Angel Ridge was focused on them. She didn't care. She loved Cole Craig. She was proud of Cole Craig. And she wanted the world to know.

"Yes!" she said clearly enough for several people to hear. "Oh, yes," she whispered for his ears alone. Word would spread through the town like a rushing wind sweeping across the shoreline. When she threw her arms around his neck and kissed him, she could have sworn she heard Dixie Ferguson say, "Well, it's about time."

The sound of applause and cheers sounded all around them. Tears filled her eyes when he pulled a velvet box out of his pocket and opened it. Nestled against the velvet lining was an exquisite square diamond in an antique silver setting.

"This ring has been in my family for generations. I hope you'll wear it."

All Josie could do was nod as the tears spilled down her cheeks. Could a person die of such happiness? She didn't deserve so many blessings.

Cole lifted the ring out of the box. "There's a story behind this. An angel's wings hold the diamond in place. It's told there's a magic in it that causes it to fit only if there's true and abiding love between the giver and the recipient."

He slid the ring on her finger and said, "A perfect fit."

He reverently touched his lips to the ring where he'd placed it on her finger, and then he gave her a kiss that seemed to seal the promise of their life together.

"When will you marry me?" he asked when he at last lifted his head.

She chewed her lower lip. As happy as she was, she wanted to savor their relationship. Wanted to learn how to be a girlfriend before she became a wife. "Would you mind if we had a long courtship?"

Cole frowned. "Define *long*."

She touched his hair. "Long enough for

your hair to grow back."

Cole ran his fingers through the shortened tresses. "I thought it made me look more respectable."

She smoothed her hand down his neck and inside his collar, around to his chest. "I like you a little disreputable."

"I like hearing you say that you like me . . ."

"How does a Christmas wedding sound?"

"Like a good way to start the New Year."

His next kiss was the stuff dreams were made of. Miss Estelee was right. You couldn't judge a book by its cover. The true love of the man who held her tightly in his arms was so much better than any love she'd ever read about in a book. It was a blessing for which she would be thankful the rest of her life.

# EPILOGUE

And that's the story of Josie and Cole. Don't it just make you want to go right out and fall in love yourself? I can tell you, they've got this whole town helpin' them plan their weddin'. Josie says she's not much for them kind of things, and well, we're all too happy to lend a hand.

And let me just say, she needs all the help she can get. That mother of hers means well, but she just about had a heart attack when we sat down to plan menus. Josie wants chicken salad sandwiches — picnic style in December — for the rehearsal dinner, and chicken and dumplins for the sit down reception dinner to serve two hundred fifty. I say, give the woman what she wants. It's her wedding. But you know how folks can be.

Cole's mother and aunt — better known around here as the sisters — what a pair! They couldn't be happier, but with what they're plannin' . . . well, let's just say that if I was Cole, I'd be real careful of that pole they expect him to ride out of the reception on! Lordy, these folks and their mountain ways. Looks dangerous to me, if you know what I mean, but to each his own. You wouldn't want to do anything that might cause bad luck for the happy couple.

Seriously, folks, I hope you enjoyed gettin' to know a few of my neighbors here in Angel Ridge. Some of us might put on airs every now and then, but at heart, we all care and watch out for one another. Well, most of us anyway. It's like family. You're not always gonna see eye to eye. You might make each other crazy from time to time — maybe even most of the time — but in the end, you're still family. Towns, like families, are important. They're at the heart of who we are. At the end of the day, I feel blessed to call Angel Ridge home.

I hope you'll see fit to come visit us again, sometime. We sure enjoyed havin' you.

# The Story of Angel Ridge

Deborah Grace Staley is pleased to share this special original short story.

## The Guardian

"He shall give His angels charge concerning you."

Matthew 4:6

*In the Wilderness, just over the mountains East of North Carolina, 1785*

"Go back . . ."

Mary dropped the berry she'd intended for her basket. "Who's there?"

She turned in a circle, but saw no one. Frowning, she returned to her task.

Her mother had sent her to pick enough blackberries for two pies. Her sigh was heavy as she plucked another berry. Her best friend, Lizzie Craig, had asked that snippety little Charlotte McKay to play hide and seek when she'd said she had to go outside the fort to gather berries.

Mary sighed again. This would take forever. She hated picking berries and working in the garden while her friends got to play. She also hated feeding the chickens, sweeping the porch, hanging the wash, and any number of the other endless chores she'd had to do since she and her family had moved to East Tennessee with her father and mother.

They'd lived in a grand home in Virginia, and there had been servants to do all the chores. Sometimes, in the early morning before she woke, Mary could swear she smelled Miss Ellie's cinnamon bread warming by the hearth oven. But then she woke, splashed water on her face, dressed and walked to the well, feet dragging, to bring in a bucket of water to wash the morning dishes after her breakfast of oatmeal had been eaten. Mary wrinkled her nose. She hated oatmeal, too.

Here, she lived in a two-room cabin that had a loft and sat at the foot of a mountain. Mother said the sunrises and sunsets were beautiful. Mary couldn't figure how that was any different from Virginia. The sun rose and set there, too. And in Virginia, all she had to do was play and go to school.

Here the chores never seemed to end, and there'd be more of those after her new baby sister arrived. Mother kept saying they'd take whatever God gave them, but God surely wanted her to have a sister.

"Mary?"

She turned again, cross this time. "Who's there?" Had that stupid old Jones boy followed her like the last time? He followed her around like a puppy.

As she looked across the clearing, the sun peeked from behind a cloud as a stranger stepped out of the tall pines and walked towards her. He was someone she'd never seen. Tall, with long golden hair that brushed his shoulders. The sun angled through the pines illuminating him in a shimmering, golden glow.

"Go home. Your papa's calling you."

Mary frowned. "No, he isn't, and he's too far away for me to hear him if he was to call me."

The big man smiled and chuckled. "You're a bright young girl, Mary, but I heard him calling you. Honest."

"How do you know my name?"

"I've known you since you came to live here on the ridge."

"But I don't know you or your name." Puzzled, Mary couldn't remember seeing him at church services or at planting and harvest time.

"Sure you do. Think . . ."

He came closer, looking straight into her eyes as he moved. The nicest feeling came across her like the one she got when she lay in the middle of the clearing in the Tall Pines when she stared up at the sky. And suddenly, she knew his name even though she was quite certain she'd never met him.

"Gabriel."

The man smiled again. "That's right."

Mary nodded. She'd known she was right.

"Let's go back to the fort now." Gabriel held out a hand towards her and turned as if to go.

"I can't go back now. Mother needs berries for two pies," she held up two fingers to emphasize her point. "She'll skin my hide if I come home without enough."

"Your basket's full, little one."

"No, it's not —"

Mary looked down and found her basket filled to the top with plump blackberries.

"How in the world?" she exclaimed.

"How 'bout if I walk back with you?"

Gabriel took the heavy basket and again held out his hand for her to take it. Slipping her hand into his big, warm one felt just like holding her papa's hand — like nothing and no one could keep her safer.

"How come I've never seen you before today, but I knew your name?"

The tall, golden man at her side smiled. "Because you're a smart girl."

Mary giggled. "I know that, silly, but that doesn't answer my question. If I'm smart, and I am, that means I should know you — which I don't — if I know your name."

Gabriel chuckled. "A very smart girl, indeed."

"And that basket was *not* full when you sneaked up on me. So, how'd it get full?"

Gabriel stopped and stooped down to look in her eyes again. "Remember your Bible lessons, little one? A basket full of berries is a blessing because your mother will make your favorite pie with them, right?"

"Well, it's papa's favorite pie, but even if it was my favorite, what's that got to do with my Bible lessons?"

"From where do blessings come?"

Mary squinted into the sun as she thought, or was that Gabriel making her squint? "Blessings come from God. It's just like the song we sing in church service. *Praise God from whom all blessings flow. Praise him all creatures here below. Praise him above ye heavenly hosts. Praise Father, Son and Holy Ghost.*"

"Yes. And you sing more beautifully than the angels in heaven."

Mary blushed at his praise.

"Go inside the fort now, Mary."

"But we're not —"

Mary blinked, then rubbed her eyes. They'd only walked a few steps, but the log fence surrounding the fort that her papa and their neighbors had built was right in front of her.

"How'd we get here so fast, Gabriel?" Mary turned in a wide circle. "Gabriel?"

"Who you bellerin' at Mary Contrary?"

Icky Elliot McGee taunted her, calling her names. He made her so mad! The least he could do was come up with something no one else would think up, but no. He said the same stupid thing every time — Mary Contrary.

"Mind your own business, Elliot McGee."

She picked up the basket of berries at her feet and, after one look at the now empty meadow, hefted the heavy burden and struggled to reach the gate. After only a couple of steps, she fell and dropped the basket. Berries scattered everywhere.

"Oh, no!"

"Mary, Mary. Clumsy, wumsy, Mary Contrary."

Elliot grabbed his sides, pointing and

laughing at her.

"You hush, Elliot!"

"Go, Mary. Leave the berries. Go to your mother. Quickly!"

Mary turned, frowning. "Gabriel?"

She'd expected to see her new friend behind her, but instead, her eyes widened at the sight of Indians racing towards the fort. Inside her head, she knew she should run, but her feet wouldn't move. She'd never been so scared.

Elliot ran to the fort without bothering to help her. Her arms and legs began to shake so bad that she couldn't get up. Tears streamed silently down her face. She wanted to cry out to her papa, her mother, or even to Gabriel, but she just couldn't make the words form on her tongue. She squeezed her eyes shut. The prayer inside her head was, "Help me, God. Please protect me."

*I'll protect you, Mary. I'll always be close by to protect you.*

"Indians!" someone shouted. "Attack! Attack! Close the gate!"

"No, wait! Mary's outside!"

It was her mother's voice, but it sounded far, far away.

Just then, an arrow flew past her, then another and another. Mary wanted to duck, but she still couldn't move, and the tears continued to fall silently down her face. She closed her eyes and prayed harder.

Then, an eerie silence surrounded her. A sweet feeling of peace and safety helped her open her eyes.

A dark shadow shielded her from the bright noonday sun. No. It wasn't a shadow. It wasn't a shadow at all. It was Gabriel, but he'd made himself huge, and great golden wings extended from his back as wide as the fence in front of the fort. The arrows that had been whizzing past her only a moment before were now blocked by Gabriel's golden wings so that they fell harmlessly to the ground, keeping her and the fort safe.

Two arms lifted her from the ground and pressed her close. It was her papa, and he ran fast to the gate while Gabriel's wings kept them both safe.

Inside the fort, the men stood silent, their guns at their sides as they stared at the awesome sight before them. Mary's papa and two others pulled the gate closed as soon as her mother got her arms around her. Mama fell to her knees, rocking back and forth while nearly squeezing the breath from her.

"My baby . . . my sweet baby . . ." She smoothed her hands over Mary's hair. "Are you all right? Are you hurt? Talk to me, please."

Mary sniffed and wiped her tears away with the back of her hand. "I spilled the berries."

Mama squeezed me harder and laughed.

"Do you see that?" I heard my papa say. "An angel. An angel is protecting us."

"It's so beautiful," Mr. Craig breathed.

"His name is Gabriel," Mary said proudly. "He helped me pick berries."

"What?" Papa asked, stooping to sweep her up into his strong arms. When he stood, she could see Gabriel, his wings still sheltering the fort, protecting them just like he'd said.

"Gabriel helped me pick the berries for Mama's pies," she said. Now that the words were coming, they tumbled out one after the other. "He helped me pick 'em quick as can be so I could come home. He got me here really fast, too. Faster than it's ever took me to walk back to the fort from the Tall Pines." She stopped then to draw in a quick breath before continuing. "Just look at him! Ain't he a sight, Papa?"

One of the men said, "They're turning back. The Indians are turning back!"

Mary smiled. "Because Gabriel was watching over us."

*"He will give his angels charge concerning you . . ."* Mama whispered the scripture.

*I'll always watch over you.*

Mary heard the words inside her head and kept them to herself like a special secret for her alone.

That very day, Mr. Craig named the new settlement high on the ridge above the little winding river, Angel Ridge.

# DIXIE FERGUSON GUIDES THE DISCRIMINATING READERS OF ONLY YOU

1. Do you have a "tell-it-like-it-is" friend like Dixie Ferguson? If not, why not? If so, what does she add to your life? What do you appreciate most about her?

2. Think about the social hierarchy in your life; at work, home, church, community. What are the "rules," either spoken or unspoken? What is socially acceptable in your world? Do you agree with those rules?

3. Josie struggled with having a career and a personal life. Can you have it all? all at one time? How do you balance the different roles in your life?

4. How important is parental/family approval to you? Do you live your life to please others? Do you have "approval addiction"? If so, why? What can you do today to begin

to change that?

5. What are your favorite childhood memories? Josie and Cole had sweet school-yard memories that shaped who they became as adults and as a couple. How did your childhood shape who you are? How are you the same today as when you were a child?

6. Josie had to deal with her obligation to Mrs. McKay. Do you do what's expected or follow your dreams?

7. Cole said, "People believe & see what they want." He was saddled with Angel Ridge's assumptions of who he was based on the lack of social standing of the "back of the ridge Craigs." On what do you base your assumptions? Looks, money, education, talent?

8. The angel statue stands in the town square & was pivotal in Josie's and Cole's romance. Miss Estelee said the angels were "workin' their magic." How did Miss Estelee play a part in the romance? Do you believe in angels? What magic have they worked in your life?

9. Poetic justice is a beautiful thing. Discuss how Josie and Cole each attained it and why it was so satisfying for them. Give an example of poetic justice in your life.

10. Family values are much talked about in Angel Ridge. Discuss Josie's family in comparison and contrast to Cole's family. Also, compare the McKay family. What are your values? How have your family's values affected your life? Which of those values are you passing on?

# ABOUT THE AUTHOR

**Deborah Grace Staley** is an award-winning author and is multi-published in short romantic fiction. Her writing awards include Duel on the Delta, the Smoky Mountain Valentine, and the DandyLine. She was honored to be a finalist in a number of contests including the Maggie, the Laurie, and the Ohio Valley Romance Writers' First Chapter Contest. She is a member Romance Writers of America and serves as President of The Society of the Purple Prose, an intrepid group of the Romantic Times Booklovers Pre-Conference Seminars. She makes her home in a circa 1867 Victorian farmhouse on five acres in East Tennessee with her husband, son, and two dogs. Deborah loves to hear from readers.

Contact her via
www.deborahgracestaley.com
or P.O. Box 672, Vonore, TN 37885

We hope you have enjoyed this Large Print book. Other Thorndike, Wheeler, Kennebec, and Chivers Press Large Print books are available at your library or directly from the publishers.

For information about current and upcoming titles, please call or write, without obligation, to:

Publisher
Thorndike Press
295 Kennedy Memorial Drive
Waterville, ME 04901
Tel. (800) 223-1244

or visit our Web site at:

http://gale.cengage.com/thorndike

OR

Chivers Large Print
published by BBC Audiobooks Ltd
St James House, The Square
Lower Bristol Road
Bath BA2 3SB
England
Tel. +44(0) 800 136919
email: bbcaudiobooks@bbc.co.uk
www.bbcaudiobooks.co.uk

All our Large Print titles are designed for easy reading, and all our books are made to last.